# DRAGON RACER

# LEGACY
## OF
# FIRE

# DRAGON RACER

# LEGACY OF FIRE

## Margaret Bateson-Hill

Catnip

CATNIP BOOKS
Published by Catnip Publishing Ltd
14 Greville Street
London EC1N 8SB

First published 2011
1 3 5 7 9 10 8 6 4 2

A CIP catalogue record for this book is available from the British Library.

ISBN 978-1-84647-121-6

Printed in Poland

www.catnippublishing.co.uk

*For my godson, Isaac Morris*

*amicus certus in re incerta cernitur*
A true friend is discerned during
an uncertain matter

# CONTENTS

# I
## MORVENA'S
# EGGS

A man's voice struggled to be heard above the howling gale and the stream of black rain that had engulfed the mountainside.

'Giovanni! Giovanni! Where are you?'

'Up here, Frank!'

A short, thick-set man, wrapped against the elements, slowly appeared from behind a projection of grey rock and pointed to a stone-marked winding path that led to his hiding place deep within the bracken, before slipping carefully from view.

A few minutes later, Frank Chatfield, owner of the Blackpool Tower Dragon Caves sank down beside his friend. He was out of breath from the climb and looking very worried.

'I got here as fast as I could when I got your call. Are you sure the dragon is about to lay her eggs?'

'Positive. Unmistakable signs,' replied Giovanni. 'Lucia saw her first, circling the summit. She said she seemed in some distress, landing on one side of the mountain and then taking off again five minutes later. But she seems to have settled now.'

'Where is she?' asked Frank.

Giovanni Balivo, owner of the Snowdonia Dragon Sanctuary, pointed up behind him to a great overhanging ledge. 'Just up there. This is as close as we can get without disturbing her.'

Frank looked up. He thought he could just make out the pointed tip of her tail.

'Did you recognise her?'

'She's a Golden Spiked-Back, and there are only three in the country. So I phoned around to see who was missing a dragon. Turns out she's called Morvena and belongs to retired cave owner Carol McKenna, who lives in Suffolk.'

'But why did she fly all the way to your mountain on the wildest night of the summer rather than lay her eggs in the safety of her own cave?' asked Frank curiously.

'I'm not sure. But earlier in the evening I climbed up onto the ledge to take her some food and found she was terribly nervous and agitated. She refused the food, which was unusual enough, but most distressing was the fact that she was muttering to herself.'

'Muttering?' Frank looked bemused. 'So what did she say?'

'Would you believe *Atishoo, Atishoo, we all fall down*?' asked Giovanni cautiously.

'What, like in the nursery rhyme?' Frank asked. 'What on earth can that mean?'

'I think she believes something or *someone* is threatening her eggs and that they will be safer here,' suggested Giovanni. 'But your guess is as good as mine.'

'But it's a threat you're taking seriously,' said Frank.

'I always take dragons seriously,' said Giovanni. 'They know things we can only guess at. Hopefully it's nothing more than the recent arrival of Carol's grandson visiting from overseas. Goodness, the Suffolk Caves must have practically been silent for the past three years with just Carol and Morvena rattling around.'

'The grandson's not going to race on Morvena, surely?' asked a horrified Frank. Egg-laying females tended to be on the slow side.

'Goodness, no!' said Giovanni. 'Carol said she'd imported a new dragon from the States for him. Didn't say what, though.'

'What about the eggs?' asked Frank.

'Carol said I was welcome to find homes to hatch them out. That with her grandson racing this season she didn't want the bother of having to egg turn as well.'

The two men fell silent. It was nearly midnight when they heard the sound they had been waiting for. The rain had stopped and the wind had dropped so there was no mistaking the long slow hiss of a female dragon igniting the fire nest for her newly laid eggs. The two men held their breath and counted thirty . . . forty . . . fifty seconds . . . and then silence.

'Shouldn't be long now,' said Frank.

'Look, there she goes!' cried Giovanni, as part of the sky disappeared into a shimmering silhouette of a dragon flying silently away.

Frank turned to Giovanni. 'Are you ready with the firebox?'

'Ready and already preset to hot,' Giovanni replied as he picked up a great leather box from the most sheltered part of their hideout.

The two men leapt into action. Frank scrambled up the ledge first, then Giovanni handed him the firebox, before climbing up to join his friend, who was shining a powerful torch into a deep hollow in the rock.

'I can just see them, but the opening's so narrow it looks like my only option is the egg scoop. Can you get it out of my bag?'

Even with their many years of rescuing dragon eggs

from precarious fire nests, Giovanni and Frank only succeeded in saving three of Morvena's eggs.

'What a shame!' sighed Frank as he secured the lid of the firebox.

Then, with great care, the two men made their way down the mountain path. It had started to rain again, making the rocks very slippery underfoot.

Late the next morning after a leisurely breakfast, cooked as usual to perfection by Giovanni's wife Lucia, Frank Chatfield put down his mug and rubbed his hands together.

'Decision time! What are you going to do with the dragon eggs?' He took out a small notebook. 'If you need suggestions, I've got a list of caves waiting for eggs and I'd like one too, if possible.'

'Take one with my gratitude for all your help last night,' said Giovanni. 'I'd never have managed without you.'

'And Brixton is a must,' insisted Lucia, peering over Frank's shoulder. 'At the last Trustee meeting we attended Agnes talked of getting an egg so that she could teach her grandson Isaac how to egg turn. She's really keen to pass on her skills, especially as Vincent had always talked about making Isaac an apprentice. And when we sounded out Joanna's parents they agreed immediately, saying Joanna would be thrilled to have someone else her own age taking on such a responsible position.'

'One egg for the new Brixton apprentice – priority then,' agreed Frank. 'I can hardly believe it has been six months since Vincent . . .'

All three of them fell silent. Even now they found it difficult to imagine that Vincent Marlowe, owner of the Brixton Caves, was dead, having sacrificed himself to save his young flyer, Joanna Morris.

'Such a wise, brave man,' exclaimed Lucia, wiping away a tear. 'Not like that wicked Marius King!' She tossed her black curls angrily. 'He's the one responsible for Vincent's death, breeding that vicious dragon without a care for anyone's safety! I'm glad he's safely locked up in prison. I hope they throw away the key! I hope . . .'

'Have the authorities decided what's going to happen to the Brighton Caves yet? I heard the WDRF are putting the lease up for sale,' interrupted Frank quickly. He understood Lucia's anger, but nothing she said could change the past.

'That's what we heard too,' said Giovanni. 'They're still clearing up after the explosion, but from what I hear the oldest, original caves are all intact. It'll be a great investment for someone. They're some of the best caves in the country.'

'And whoever buys it will need dragon eggs,' said

Frank, 'which will be good for me. Although it doesn't help us decide where this last one should go.'

'Names in a hat?' suggested Lucia.

'Why not,' laughed Frank. 'It's as fair as anything else.'

Lucia copied down the names of the caves from Frank's notebook, folded them up and dropped them into a bowl. Giving it a quick swirl, she handed it to her husband.

Giovanni pulled one out. 'And the final egg goes to . . . Hull University Dragon Racing Society!'

## 2
# MOVING
## ON

'Agnes, it's here!' an excited voice echoed down the long
rock-hewn passages of the Brixton Dragon Caves, until
finally its owner burst into the Egg Turner's office.

'Good morning, Joanna. Yes, you may come in,
although how many times do I have to tell you that
it's polite to knock first?'

'Sorry, Agnes,' said Joanna, flicking her plaits from
side to side excitedly. 'It's just that I wanted to be the
person to tell you!'

'Tell me what? That you left Mr Chatfield and the
egg waiting on the doorstep?'

'Of course not,' said Joanna. 'Spiky Mike is with
him – they immediately started discussing all sorts of
technical things, so I left them to take the lift and ran
down the stairs. I can beat the lift by a whole minute
now. It's part of my keep-fit regime.'

Agnes Thomas smiled down at Joanna's flushed face. No one would ever guess that this excited girl was World Champion of dragon racing and owner of the Brixton Caves. It was moments such as these that made the old woman stop and pause. Could she ever forget the wonderful day that had changed all their lives, when she and her dearest friend Vincent Marlowe had hatched the Silver Spiked-Back dragon Excelsior in the silver fire of alchemy? And it was the same silver fire that had saved Joanna's life. Perhaps that was why the bond between Joanna and Excelsior was the most extraordinary she had ever witnessed in all her years of dragon racing. Here they were, the champions she and Vincent had dreamed of, only now Vincent wasn't here to share the reality. Agnes would still walk past his study door half-expecting to hear his voice call out to tell her some piece of news that had amused or intrigued him.

November would see the beginning of the new racing season and that was only a couple of months away. How would they manage without him? Of course it was exciting that Afra and Hannibal had joined them from Marius King's old Brighton Caves as trainer and flyer of their new dragon, Aurora, but there were bound to be tensions and niggling jealousies . . .

Agnes sighed. She understood just how competitive

the racing world could be. Last season Joanna and Hannibal had flown for rival teams. What worried Agnes now was that as the oldest member of the Brixton Caves, everyone would turn to her to solve their problems.

'All I can say, Vincent, is I'll do my best to guide them! But I fear I'm getting too old for this. I should be retiring back home to the Caribbean like I promised myself when I was younger!'

At least the arrival of the new egg was an area in which Agnes felt confident passing on her expertise.

'Don't just stand there, Joanna, go and call Afra and Hannibal. They are busy training, but I know they'll want to see Mr Chatfield too.'

Joanna ran down the low-arched passage that led to the dragon caves, popped her head round the ancient wooden door of Aurora's cave and delivered the news to her colleagues, before throwing open the door to the neighbouring cave.

'XL . . . Excelsior!' she called. 'It's here! The dragon egg is here!'

She quickly turned up one of the oil lamps, making strange shadows leap off the darkness of the walls. A soft halo of golden light illuminated the silver dragon stretched along the cave floor. Excelsior didn't stir but his sleepy voice called out in a soft metallic rasp, 'So that's why I haven't had my breakfast yet when I know Aurora's already had hers! Just the thought of a new dragon egg and you're already forgetting about me!'

The dragon half opened his fire-bright eyes to see if his flyer was showing any sympathy to his plight.

'I bet when it hatches it'll be a Crimson Flame dragon like Ariadne and she (it's bound to be a girl) will be all pink and pretty and you'll fly off on her with your friend Mouse and do girly things!'

'You know that Silver Spiked-Backs are my favourite and I could *never* want to fly another dragon other than you,' said Joanna affectionately, running her finger along the smooth shiny scales of her dragon's powerful neck. 'And I certainly didn't know you hadn't been fed this morning. I thought Isaac was doing all the breakfasts now.'

Joanna left Excelsior with an extra-big breakfast and hurried back to Agnes's office. She was annoyed that the Egg Turner's grandson had forgotten to feed her dragon and was all ready to complain, but when she got there, she found everyone engrossed in listening to how Frank and Giovanni had rescued Morvena's eggs. They all watched in suspense as Frank Chatfield unzipped a padded holdall that lay waiting on Agnes's desk and took out the dragon-egg carrier.

'We are indebted to you, Frank,' said Agnes.

'Both to you and Giovanni. I know how many other requests there must have been.'

'I really can't think of a better home for it,' said Frank.

'Can I come with you to the Nursery Caves and watch you do the first turn, Agnes?' Joanna asked excitedly. 'I'm really looking forward to seeing you begin. Do you remember how I used to come and watch you turn Aurora?'

'You know we can't start until Isaac gets here,' replied Agnes.

'Why not?' asked Joanna, looking puzzled. 'Come on, don't let's wait, he can see it tomorrow.'

'*See* it?' laughed Agnes. 'I think people waste far too much time watching. With egg turning you learn best if you just "do" it. Why, when I hatched my first egg, I wasn't even supervised! I was just given the egg-turning manual and told to follow the instructions. But I want Isaac to have a formal training – to serve a proper apprenticeship.'

'An apprentice Egg Turner?' said Joanna, stunned by the news. 'You mean Isaac's going to turn the egg . . . and hatch out the new dragon? No one told me!'

'Hey, what's the big deal, Jo?' drawled Hannibal.

Joanna looked over to her fellow flyer. He was leaning casually back in Agnes's easy chair. The dragons had named him $H_2O$ – cool but essential, like water. As ever, he was living up to his name in his designer jeans and trainers, and out of racing season he was wearing his hair in a wonderful Afro. He added a touch of glamour to the team and although it had been Joanna's idea that he should join the Brixton Caves as a flyer, she still felt slightly in awe of him.

'We thought you might be pleased to have someone else your age taking an active role,' snapped Spiky Mike, Joanna's trainer. 'He's eager to learn and he's very respons—'

'Oh no he's not!' interrupted Joanna, indignantly. 'He didn't give Excelsior his breakfast this morning.'

'Hold on a minute, *young lady*!' Spiky Mike glared at her. 'Last night I overheard you insist that *you* wanted to be responsible for that. Isaac was incredibly nice about it, considering your tone of voice. Does this mean Excelsior hasn't been fed this morning?'

Joanna scowled. How could she have forgotten? The evening before she'd come into Excelsior's cave only to find Isaac talking to her dragon as he fed him. He was laughing out loud at some joke. When Joanna had asked what was so funny the pair of them had both laughed again and Isaac had said, 'You won't get it, Jo, you're a girl.'

Joanna had been furious. Who did Isaac think he was, acting like *he* and Excelsior were best buddies! She'd put her arm firmly around her dragon's neck and said as icily as she could, 'I'll feed Excelsior from now on. He's *my* dragon. And by the way, my name's Joanna. Jo is for my *friends*, who let me in on their jokes.'

Now, embarrassed at having been caught out in front of everyone, Joanna snapped back at Spiky Mike, 'Don't worry I've fed Excelsior, OK?'

'Isaac can continue feeding Aurora as much as he likes,' said Hannibal, trying to lighten the mood. 'It's real hard work, all that feeding and cleaning up afterwards. Flying is easy in comparison.'

But Spiky Mike was not going to let his young flyer off so lightly. 'Have you cleaned up yet, Joanna? No? Then go and do it now! I don't want dirty food troughs in *these* caves! And Isaac will do all the feeding from now on.'

Joanna was in the middle of scrubbing out Excelsior's feeding trough when Afra came to help her.

'Feel like telling me what all that was about?' she asked cautiously.

'Excelsior's *my* dragon – I should look after him. And . . .' Joanna was scrubbing the feeding trough far more vigorously than she needed.

'And?' Afra waited.

'What if I don't want Isaac to learn how to egg turn?'

Afra looked rather taken aback. 'Don't you think Isaac deserves a chance, especially when he's always here doing the muckiest and hardest jobs . . .'

'Exactly!' interrupted Joanna. 'He's *always* here, buzzing round *doing* things and . . . I don't want things to change . . . I mean Agnes is our Egg Turner and . . .'

Joanna didn't get chance to finish because Spiky Mike suddenly burst into the cave. 'Haven't you finished yet?'

'Mike! There's no need to shout,' smiled Afra, going over and slipping her arm through his.

'Actually I was just coming to tell you that Frank's about to leave. I thought you'd like to say goodbye,' replied Spiky Mike more calmly. 'By the way, Joanna, he's got a parcel for you from Mouse.'

'Oh, that must be the top she promised I could borrow. Fantastic!' said Joanna, brightening up immediately. Mouse was Frank Chatfield's youngest daughter and Joanna's best friend.

'Ooh, I could ask Frank to take back one of mine. Can I nip home to get one?'

'Don't be ridiculous,' snapped Spiky Mike. 'Frank would miss his train. You'll just have to post it tomorrow.'

Feeling slightly deflated, Joanna followed the others up the corridor. She found herself wishing that Afra was her trainer instead. If only Spiky Mike would treat her with half the understanding that his girlfriend did. You would have thought that now she was World Champion he'd be more relaxed, but he was *still* as spiky as ever!

'If only you were still here, Vincent,' sighed Joanna as she walked past the closed door that marked the Alchemist's study. 'It's not the same without you.'

Mouse's parcel cheered her up considerably. Not only had she sent the promised T-shirt, but also a pair of the brightest tangerine socks Joanna had ever seen – a souvenir of Mouse's first visit to watch Blackpool FC. She immediately went to show them to Excelsior, knowing he would just love them.

'I do wish I could see Mouse more often,' Joanna sighed to her dragon. 'Much as I love watching her and Ariadne perform their acrobatics, I'd like them to race. Perhaps Spiky Mike will let us go up to Blackpool to watch Hannibal and Aurora in the Novice Race in November and I can see her then. I mean, as Cave Owner, I should get an invitation to attend.'

'If Spiky Mike says no, we could sneak out of the caves anyway and fly up to Blackpool on our own,' suggested Excelsior enthusiastically. 'You could stay with Mouse and I'm sure Ariadne would love to have me as a cave guest for a few days.'

'Imagine the look on Spiky Mike's face when he discovered we had gone!' laughed Joanna, giving her dragon a quick hug.

When it came to it, Joanna couldn't bring herself to watch Isaac turn the egg. The truth was she hated him being in the caves. She hadn't minded when he'd just helped out occasionally, in fact she'd hardly noticed him being there, but now he seemed to be there all the time. To make matters worse, Agnes never seemed to stop talking about him. *Isaac this! Isaac that!* Just because he was her grandson it didn't entitle him to be in the caves *or* to be the next Egg Turner. And why had no one asked Joanna what *she* wanted?

*These are my caves!* she wanted to shout as she went off to find Spiky Mike, who was in the library looking at one of Agnes's egg-turning manuals.

'I'm going home,' she told him, rubbing her head. 'I've got a headache.'

But her trainer didn't even look up.

Joanna fumed inwardly. Not even a 'I hope you feel better'. Did he ever see her as a person?

'Before you go,' he said, still unable to take his eyes away from the manual, 'there are some forms I need your parents to sign. They're in a large brown envelope in my office. Whatever you do don't lose them or you won't be racing this season!'

Joanna stomped up the corridor to Spiky Mike's office muttering all the horrible names she could think of, all the while hoping she wouldn't bump into either Agnes or Afra. She knew Agnes would be hurt she wasn't staying to watch the egg turning and that Afra wouldn't be taken in by her excuse of a headache. Still, at least they both treated her like a human being.

*Large brown envelope?* she said to herself looking at Spiky Mike's desk. It was swamped in half-written envelopes, forms, timetables and bills.

'Tut, tut, Spiky Mike,' she said aloud, finding the envelope after a rather self-satisfied hunt. 'I really think we should clean up after ourselves. We don't want such an untidy desk in *these* caves.'

# 3
## THE
# APPRENTICE

Isaac Ankama grabbed his school bag and ran to the bus stop just in time to catch the bus. He definitely did not want to be late on this particular evening. He was feeling quite nervous. Everyone in the caves was bound to be at the egg turning – including Jo, sorry, *Joanna* Morris. He sighed. Why did she always have to make things so difficult for him?

So some pretty traumatic things had happened to her in the previous year, but some fantastic ones had too. How many people even got to fly a dragon let alone *race* one and become champion of the world! And couldn't she see that *everyone* in the caves missed Vincent – Isaac's grandma more than anyone? He thought just how much older and slower Agnes had been since her friend's death. He worried about her, which was part of the reason he was working extra hard in the caves, just to make her life easier. But now there was all this talk about wanting to fulfil Vincent's wish about making him an apprentice!

It had been a dream come true when the Trustees had asked him to become Apprentice Egg Turner for the Brixton Caves! Ever since he'd first visited them as a little boy he'd loved everything about them: the strange silence so far underground when cars and lorries were hurtling by overhead; the soft golden glow of the oil lamps that illuminated the darkness; as for the dragons – those glorious winged creatures took his breath away. Now he was going to hatch one. For fourteen months he'd turn the egg in the fire. He'd feel the egg grow heavy with dragon until one day it would burst from its shell. Who knows, perhaps it would become a champion like Excelsior? And he'd get to name it. His grandma liked names from literature but he'd name his dragons after scientists and mathematicians. Ptolemy! Galileo! Copernicus! He could see them in his mind's eye racing towards the finish line.

Too late Isaac realised he'd missed his stop. Annoyed at his own stupidity, he jumped off the bus and ran full speed back down the road to the town hall, glancing up at the clock as he went. He was late! He pushed though the doors of the back entrance, jumping down the steps two at a time and crashed straight into Joanna, who fell heavily against the wall.

'Sorry,' he gasped, out of breath. 'I wasn't expecting to meet anyone.'

'Obviously!' replied Joanna curtly, brushing off Isaac's attempt to help her up.

'But what are you doing here?' asked Isaac, surprised to see her.

'What am *I* doing here!' snapped Joanna. '*I* am minding my own business and certainly *not* knocking people off their feet.'

'Come on, Joanna, you know that's not what I meant,' replied Isaac. 'I mean, why aren't you in the caves for the egg turning?' A moment of doubt suddenly flashed across his face. 'Mr Chatfield did come, didn't he?'

Joanna didn't reply, she simply pushed past him as if to continue up the stairs. Then she stopped a few steps higher up and turned, so that now she was looking down at him.

'Of course he came! But *I* can't stay. I've got a headache and now a sore arm.' She winced as she rubbed her elbow. 'I think it's bruised and it really hurts.' Then she continued up the stairs without another backward glance or a goodbye.

'Yeah, see you, Miss High and Mighty Jo*anna*,' said Isaac watching her disappear through the door. He continued more slowly down the steps. 'Instead of being rude why not be honest and just say you don't want me to become the Egg Turner. Well, tough luck, I will be! And I'll be so good that you'll just have to admit it. So go on home with your headache and sore arm. At least I won't have to put up with your pathetic comments.'

It was with a great deal of pride that Agnes Thomas, the Egg Turner of the Brixton Caves, led her grandson Isaac to the Nursery Caves. Whilst they were the smallest caves in the Brixton complex – some little more than a hollow in the rock face – they were also the oldest, having been discovered hundreds of years ago by the first Dragon Lord of the Brixton Caves. The small oil lamps had been turned down low, giving the caves a soft, warm, dreamy feel as if time were standing still.

As he followed his grandma, Isaac soon forgot about Joanna's outburst. All that mattered was the task he was about to undertake – the turning of a dragon's egg. From this moment until the day it hatched, it would be his responsibility. As he put on the fireproof gloves and opened the firebox in its hollow in the wall ready to receive the egg, he was aware of people standing behind him and watching with anticipation and excitement.

'It's time!' announced Agnes proudly. 'Transfer the egg from its travelling box and place it in the firebox.'

Spiky Mike ceremoniously stepped forward with the box containing the dragon's egg. 'Here you go, Isaac. Ready when you are.'

Isaac undid the catch and opened the box. There it lay in a ring of blue flame – Morvena's egg. Pale gold in colour, it was larger than he'd expected; about the size of small ostrich egg. He picked it up firmly, and transferred it quickly but carefully into the open firebox, making sure to give it half a turn as he did. Although he would have been happy to study the faint, delicate markings on its shell, Isaac knew that it was essential to maintain a constant temperature at this delicate stage. He quickly shut the firebox and fastened its clasp, checking the temperature dial on the front was correct. Finally he stepped back and gave a huge sigh of relief. Yes! He'd done it.

Isaac turned to look at his grandma. She gave a little nod of pride and then said, 'Time to fill in the register, Apprentice Egg Turner.'

# 4
## WAKE UP,
# JOANNA!

After her training session in the park the following morning, Joanna arrived at the caves feeling much better. Until she saw Isaac sitting in Agnes's office, filling in the egg-turning register with Agnes's own fountain pen. The old woman was looking over her grandson's shoulder, watching every stroke.

'You've begun to note down some of the markings on the eggshell already,' Agnes smiled approvingly as Isaac closed the book.

Sitting there side by side, Joanna could see the family resemblance so clearly. They had the same high forehead and narrow face, although Isaac was darker than his grandma. And even though he was taller and slimmer he leaned over the desk in exactly the same way, as if concentrating all his attention on what he was doing. As Joanna watched them through the glass panel in the door she just couldn't squash down the flash of irritation that swept over her. *Mr Perfect Isaac*, she thought as she flung open the door without knocking.

'We're back,' she said abruptly, without greeting either of them. 'Excelsior's in his cave, waiting for breakfast. I'm off for my shower.'

Joanna closed the door quickly before either Agnes or Isaac could say anything. She intended to take an extra long time in the shower just to make sure she didn't have to talk to Isaac before he left to go to school.

'What took you so long?' asked Excelsior when she finally returned to his cave. 'I'm dying to know what you think of my new trick.'

'New trick?' Joanna sat down beside Excelsior. She was all attention.

'Did you not see when I changed direction really fast? I was chasing Aurora round the oak tree. I decided to go the other way and trick her, and somehow I span around on the spot.'

'You span on the spot? Sounds amazing! So what did you do?'

'I wasn't sure at first, but now the more I think of it the more brilliant it becomes,' exclaimed Excelsior. 'I can't think why I hadn't thought of it before!'

'Thought of what?'

'It's quite simple really – although actually it happened quite by accident.'

'XL, you're not telling me *anything*!' said Joanna exasperated by her dragon's inability to give her any concrete information.

'It's hard to explain,' said Excelsior. 'I somehow gathered up the fire in my belly and spun it into a fireball and the next thing I knew I was facing the other way. I want to try it again now. Quick, before Spiky Mike comes in.'

Joanna didn't need asking twice. She climbed up onto Excelsior's back and, placing her cheek against his, she began the simple routine of asking the questions that would take her into the mind-blend with her dragon, allowing them to communicate as one. Although she had asked the questions more times than she could remember, Joanna still found the moment of transition a moment of wonder and strangeness.

*What are you?*
*I am a dragon*
*What is your name?*
*My name is Excelsior*
*What type of dragon are you?*
*I am a Silver Spiked-Back dragon*
*Shall we mind-blend?*
*Yes*

As Joanna's thoughts melted into those of her dragon's she immediately experienced his impatient excitement and need to show her what he had learned. Following his lead, she concentrated all thoughts on the gentle regular pulse of fire in Excelsior's belly as he lay still on the cave floor.

'OK,' said Excelsior. 'On three let's gather the fire into a ball, hold it for three and then let go.'

'One, two, three . . . hold and . . .'

Both dragon and girl felt the rush of fire as it spun round and round Excelsior's belly. All Joanna could hear was the sound of her own blood pounding in her ears and her heart thumping wildly in her chest . . .

'Joanna? Joanna? Wake up!'

Joanna pulled open her eyes. Isaac was staring anxiously down at her and she realised she was lying on the floor of the cave, next to Excelsior. Her head was spinning and she had a cracking headache.

'Who . . . what happened . . . ? Excelsior?'

'Joanna, it's me, Isaac. Are you OK?'

'What the . . . ?' Spiky Mike pushed past Isaac. 'Call the doctor, quick.'

'What on earth were the pair of you playing at?' Spiky Mike asked Joanna as soon as the doctor had gone, assuring them the worst that had happened was a small scrape to Joanna's hand.

The pair of them were now sitting in Spiky Mike's office surrounded by cardboard boxes of paper – Spiky Mike's attempt at tidying up.

'We were experimenting,' said Joanna excitedly. 'After training this morning Excelsior learned that he could instantly change direction by gathering up the fire in his belly, then spinning it so that it becomes a fireball.'

'Ingenious!' exclaimed Spiky Mike, all attention, his usual irritable self gone in an instant as he realised that Excelsior had discovered some amazing trick that was going to give his flying team the advantage that season. Pulling his chair closer he leaned towards Joanna. 'Go on,' he grinned.

Joanna knew he was as intrigued by the idea as Excelsior was.

'We tried spinning the fire in a mind-blend and the next thing I knew I was on the floor.'

'Which is where Isaac found you.'

Joanna ignored this comment.

'Luckily for you he was on a late start. Didn't need to be in school till elev—'

'What do you mean luckily?' interrupted Joanna indignantly. 'I'm not hurt! And it was hardly the rescue of the century.'

'But you *could* have been hurt, so don't do it again unless I'm there. Afra and Hannibal take Aurora off to

Wales to prepare for the Novice Race in a few weeks time. It will give us the perfect opportunity to work on this in secret.'

Joanna looked at Spiky Mike in disbelief. 'In secret? But don't you and Afra share notes?'

'On certain things, but I don't expect Afra to tell me everything she does in training.'

'But she's your girlfriend – isn't that like going behind her back?'

'Wake up, Joanna! Hannibal and Aurora want to beat you more than anything. Why do you think they spend so much time watching you train? I would be failing in my job if I gave away all our secrets. Come on – it's healthy competition. Don't believe me? Then I suggest you go and have a chat with Excelsior and ask him why he was experimenting with dragon fire in the first place!'

Joanna listened in stunned amazement. Had she been asleep for the last couple of months? Everybody but her was already training in earnest for the next racing season. There they all were, making plans, watching each other, and thriving on the natural rivalry between the two teams. How could she have missed it?

Joanna took her sandwiches and sat in the gardens opposite the town hall. It was lovely to sit in the sun and do nothing but watch everybody hurrying by.

Just the space she needed to gather her own thoughts.

'Joanna?' The quiet voice behind her made her start. She didn't want to turn round, but she had to.

'Agnes!'

'I haven't really seen you this morning and I was wondering why.'

Joanna felt her face flush but she tried to smile and act as naturally as possible.

'XL and I were experimenting with the mindblend and I fell off. I cut my hand slightly, but it's nothing to worry about.'

'I'm glad you're all right,' said Agnes gently, 'but it doesn't explain why you were so rude earlier and why you didn't stay to watch the egg turning last night.'

Joanna could hear the upset in Agnes's voice. She didn't answer at first but stared at the long line of cars waiting for the traffic lights to change.

'*You're* the Egg Turner at the Brixton Caves, not Isaac,' she said at last.

'Look at me, Joanna,' replied Agnes. Something in her voice made Joanna turn to look at her friend.

Agnes smiled sadly. 'Joanna, I'm getting old. I *am* old. These last few months . . . they have affected me even more than I thought. Now don't look worried. I'm not going to disappear just yet but I've had to ask myself some long hard questions. What if I fall ill next week or next month? Who will egg turn for the caves then? I want . . . I *need* to pass on my skills while I still can. Isn't it better that I choose how? My grandson Isaac is a natural Egg Turner. He's patient, careful, the dragons like him . . . and Vincent wanted it. You don't really mind, do you?'

Joanna hesitated. What she really wanted to say was mixed up in a great jumble of thoughts. *I don't want things to change. I don't want you to get old. And I miss Vincent. Spiky Mike is bossier than ever and now Isaac's always buzzing around doing things and no one tells me anything or asks what I think.* But she couldn't.

'I feel like I don't matter,' was all she could think to say.

'Goodness, we're doing all this for you! And not just for this year and the next – but so that in five, six years' time you'll have caves worth owning. But I hear what you say . . .' Agnes hesitated, then sighing she continued, 'I might as well tell you now that we've made another decision. It's only just been finalised, so don't get cross.'

'What?' asked Joanna nervously.

'Although I've been teaching you since Vincent died – well, I think you know it was always just a temporary measure.'

'Yes?' said Joanna hesitantly. Suddenly it dawned on her. 'You mean a new tutor? When?'

'Next week,' continued Agnes quickly. 'We've already missed the first week of term, but we thought it better to wait for the right person and last night he phoned to accept the position.'

'He?' asked Joanna.

'His name is Ambrose Hogan. And he's an old friend of Spiky Mike's family.'

*Oh*, thought Joanna. *Is that good . . . or bad?*

# 5
## THE
## NEW TUTOR

Mr Hogan was not at all like Joanna had imagined. She'd been expecting a clone of Spiky Mike wearing scruffy jeans, trainers and baggy T-shirt. Instead, Mr Hogan could have been any of the teachers at her brother's school in his blue shirt, black jacket and corduroy trousers. He had short brown hair and a pair of tortoiseshell glasses and was wearing a tie. Spiky Mike *never* wore a tie.

As Joanna and Spiky Mike came into the library, he put down a book he'd been reading on the table.

'Ambrose!' Spiky Mike walked over and shook his hand enthusiastically. 'It's been . . .'

'Seven years,' smiled Mr Hogan. 'I've been teaching in the Far East for the last three, but eventually the call of home gets the better of us all and here I am back in the good old UK!'

'Joanna, come and meet Mr Hogan!' said Spiky Mike. 'Like Vincent, Mr Hogan is both a scientist and a linguist.' To Joanna's surprise, her new tutor seemed to have twirled on the spot and was zooming towards her.

'Ooh!' she couldn't help but blurt out. 'You've got a wheelchair! Oh, Mr Hogan, I'm sorry I . . .'

'. . . am a young person caught unawares who states the obvious. No need to be embarrassed. Come and sit down.' He turned back to Spiky Mike. 'I've drawn up a provisional timetable and, as you requested, added Latin to the curriculum.'

'I'm starting Latin?' asked Joanna, nervously. 'Isn't it difficult?'

'No more than anything else, I promise you,' said Mr Hogan. 'As so many of the books here are in Latin, it would be a shame if you couldn't read them when you're older. Is that all right with you, Joanna?'

'You're asking *me*?' replied Joanna, already liking her new teacher. 'Yes, that's fine and I know Vincent would have wanted it. But we'll go slowly, won't we?'

'One step at a time,' smiled Mr Hogan. 'And as there's no time like the present, or as the Romans would have said, *carpe diem*. Let's start now!'

'What's your new teacher like then?' asked Excelsior

when Joanna arrived in his cave at the end of her first day. 'Did you learn anything new and amazing?'

'Oh, Excelsior,' said Joanna excitedly. 'I've started learning Latin. I'm a *puella* – that's a girl, and you are a *draco* – that's a dragon, and the word for fire is *ignis* and *volare* means to fly. Mr Hogan's teaching me so I can read some of Vincent's old books. Imagine that! Perhaps I can learn to be an alchemist like the old Dragon Lords!'

'So I take it you like him then,' said Excelsior.

'Yup!' said Joanna. 'And he's taught children in Japan, Australia and Korea. He obviously likes old books because he kept going over to the shelves and saying that Vincent had a really fantastic collection. He thought some of the books must be over two hundred years old! And he wanted to know which ones Vincent had used when he taught me and if he had a favourite. But I didn't know. He's very keen to come and meet you too, XL. He said it was years since he's seen a dragon and that he's certainly never met a supreme champion.'

'I've been finding out interesting stuff too!' said Excelsior when he could get a word in. 'Whilst I was having my lunch, Isaac told me about the new egg.'

Joanna was torn between curiosity of hearing about the new egg and not wanting to hear about Isaac. Curiosity won.

'What's it like?' she asked as casually as she could.

'Ooh,' Excelsior continued enthusiastically, 'it's golden with small whitey-silver speckles. It sounds beautiful, doesn't it?'

'It does,' agreed Joanna, admitting she desperately wanted to see it. Perhaps she should just swallow her pride and go and watch that evening. She was just about to ask Excelsior's opinion when there was a knock on the door to the cave.

When she opened the door, there was her teacher and – surprise, surprise – Isaac.

'Ah, Joanna, Isaac has kindly agreed to show me around the caves before the egg turning and I so wanted to meet Excelsior that we came here first.'

'Of course,' said Joanna, 'come in.' She moved to one side to let Mr Hogan's chair through, but as Isaac followed him she said, 'Don't worry, Isaac, I'll take Mr Hogan round the rest of the caves – you must be so busy with feeding and getting ready for the egg turning.'

Isaac gave a shrug. 'If you like.'

Joanna watched gleefully as he made his way down the corridor to Aurora's cave to start the evening feeding programme. She turned to her teacher with a huge smile.

'Meet Excelsior, Supreme Champion!' She couldn't help bursting with pride as her dragon drew himself up to full height and let out a small blast of fire.

'He's showing off for you,' laughed Joanna.

Suddenly she stopped. Mr Hogan seemed to have turned very pale and Joanna could have sworn that just for an instant a look of blind panic had flashed across his face. But it had only been an instant and now he was laughing too and had wheeled his chair forward to give Excelsior a pat.

'I'd forgotten what glorious creatures they are. Now then, can you remember what the Latin word for dragon is?' But before she could answer, Isaac came back with Excelsior's supper.

'Feed time,' he said and slopped the food into the trough. 'And, Joanna, Grandma said she hoped you would stay and watch the egg turning tonight.'

Joanna heard Excelsior give a little snort behind her and she felt herself blush as Mr Hogan looked questioningly at her.

'Don't you normally stay; I thought you'd be really keen to learn all aspects of dragon racing? Agnes has already promised me that I can look at the original egg-turning manuscript. She told me how important it was in the birth of Excelsior.'

Everyone looked at Excelsior, who responded with a dramatic flutter of his wings, before he returned to eating his supper.

Mr Hogan turned to Isaac. 'Your grandma told me that you're already studying Latin at school. Why not come and join us for our class? I'll timetable it for last thing on Monday afternoons to give you time to get here.'

Isaac looked really pleased. 'Thanks, Mr Hogan, I'd love to.'

Joanna could hardly believe what she was hearing. Isaac in her Latin class! Was there no escaping him? She turned away and pretended to see whether Excelsior had finished his meal.

Since her opinion of Mr Hogan had just sunk to zero, she said in her *sweetest* voice, 'Mr Hogan, I don't think we've got enough time to see the rest of the caves before the egg turning.'

'That's a shame, but there's always tomorrow,' said Mr Hogan. 'Let's get going then.' Spinning his wheelchair towards the door enthusiastically, he called out, 'Lead the way, Isaac!'

'I'll be there in a minute,' called Joanna as they left the cave. 'I'm just saying goodnight to Excelsior.' But as soon as she was on her own she let out a giant groan. 'Oh, Excelsior, I can't wait till we start racing – it's the only way I'm going to get away from that boy!'

'Don't you worry,' snorted Excelsior. 'Once we've mastered fireballing, no one and I mean *no one* will be able to catch us!'

# 6

# FIREBALLING

Much to Joanna's annoyance, Isaac was really good at Latin. A few lessons were all it took to show that not only could he could reel off long lists of words, but he understood how and why the Latin words changed their endings – something she hadn't a clue about. Mr Hogan was delighted.

'Why, Isaac, with this extra tuition you'll be translating *Ova Draconum* by Christmas!' he marvelled. 'I'll ask Agnes to start copying out the text from the original so we can have a working copy to study. Obviously the original is too valuable for everyday use.'

Joanna was horrified. She hated the thought of Isaac poring over even a *copy* of Vincent's precious manuscript. But there was nothing she could say since Vincent had left the original to Agnes. Still, at least the most valuable documents – all of Vincent's books on alchemy – were in his study and she would jolly well insist they stayed there until she was eighteen and the caves were properly hers . . .

'Joanna! Have you been listening to a word I've been saying?' Mr Hogan broke into Joanna's thoughts with a jump. 'Look, you've hardly started with that translation.'

If she was floundering in her Latin classes, things were taking a much more exciting turn in her flying lessons. The morning Afra, Hannibal and Aurora left for Wales, Spiky Mike arrived in Excelsior's cave saying, 'I've looked up fireballing in the WDRF book of rules and regulations and I can't find any reference to it at all, which means it's not a banned or illegal technique. So we've got six weeks until the beginning of the season to nail it.'

'Are we going to try fireballing this morning?' Joanna immediately looked across at Excelsior, who seemed just as excited as she was.

Spiky Mike didn't reply. Instead he went over to Excelsior and stood deep in thought for a couple of minutes just looking at the dragon. Joanna shifted restlessly from foot to foot, desperate for him to reply. But Spiky Mike would not be rushed. When he finally did turn back towards Joanna she thought she'd never seen him look so unsure about anything.

She also knew by the way he kept glancing back at Excelsior that he was very excited.

'Look, I'm making this up as I go along, so bear with me. First take Excelsior down into the large training cave whilst I get my camera and laptop. I'm going to video this fireballing so we can see what happens in detail.'

Joanna and Excelsior couldn't get down to the large training cave fast enough and the pair of them waited impatiently for Spiky Mike to set up the tripod and camcorder.

'OK,' he said at last. 'Let's go.'

As Joanna asked the questions that would allow her to blend her thoughts with her dragon's she was half aware that Spiky Mike had a second camera and was walking slowly around them. She tried to ignore him and concentrated instead on the spinning fire that was whirling faster and faster all around her . . .

. . . and then she was on the floor staring up at her trainer, who was looking completely baffled but concerned. Joanna immediately jumped up to prove she was fine.

'It's OK, I'm not hurt. Did you see what happened? Why did I fall off?'

Spiky Mike looked from flyer to dragon. Excelsior's wings were quivering.

'I haven't a clue what you did, but I think I've

51

caught it on camera!' He took out his laptop and plugged in the camera. 'I'll slow it down so we can watch it frame by frame.'

Spiky Mike clicked the mouse and a slow-motion image of Excelsior with Joanna on his back appeared on the screen. Joanna gasped. Excelsior was spinning round and round like a street dancer performing some fancy move. Even slowed down it seemed to happen in the blink of an eye.

Her trainer gave a low whistle. 'He's turning so fast, no wonder you fell off. Try it again, Jo, only this time, get Excelsior to spin his fire very slowly.'

'Actually, JoJo, try going into the centre of the fire itself,' said Excelsior. 'I think you're falling off because you're just bouncing off the edge.'

'OK, XL, but still not too fast or I'll be covered in bruises,' whispered Joanna as she climbed up again onto the powerful silver-scaled back.

This time the fireball was much slower, but even so its power took Joanna's breath away. Deep within the mind-blend she allowed Excelsior's thoughts to pull her into the fire itself. Silver flames twisted and curled around her. They were alive. She could sense their power, their force. This fire *was* her dragon; Excelsior's very life force. And Excelsior was a racing dragon . . . suddenly she caught his desire and love of speed.

'Go, XL, go!' she cried, allowing herself to be carried deeper and faster into the twist of the spiralling silver flames. In an instant she was in the eye of the fire storm where nothing moved at all. She laughed. It was so easy! From this point of calm she could move in any direction she chose.

'Let's fly too, XL,' said Joanna excitedly.

'My thoughts exactly,' agreed Excelsior, as he leapt up into the air. 'Although I wish we had the camera to film Spiky Mike's face as we do!'

Spiky Mike could only watch in stunned awe, his camera hanging idle in his hand.

'Don't mention this to anyone and I mean *anyone*,' insisted Spiky Mike. 'It's so extraordinary that I want to think how we can best use it to our advantage. It almost makes me feel sorry for the competition. So promise me not a whisper – not even to your mum and dad.'

But Joanna was too excited. She hadn't felt like this since she and Excelsior had broken the speed record. She *had* to tell someone. As soon as her studies were over she found herself standing outside Vincent's study. He would have been the first person she would have told. So why not now? She touched the door handle and hesitated. She'd put this off for so long. She hadn't been inside Vincent's study since that awful moment when they realised he'd been kidnapped by

Marius King. She could still vividly see the wreckage of glass and papers strewn across the floor and Vincent's overthrown chair all smashed to pieces. She remembered the day Agnes had announced she was going to tidy up. No one had said anything and when she came out nobody asked her about it. As far as Joanna knew nobody had been in since. Now was a good time.

She turned the handle and felt the door open under her touch. She slipped quickly inside and closed the door behind her. It was completely dark but Joanna couldn't bring herself to turn on the light. She felt her way slowly across the room to the fireplace where she had first seen Vincent's silver fire the day she walked in unannounced. He had been heating a small tube of liquid. She hadn't understood then its significance – only now did she understand that it had saved her life.

'*Aqua regia,*' she said softly to herself, 'the elixir of life – *my* life! Oh, Vincent, I wish you were here to see how Excelsior has learned to spin the fire. We're going to be so fast this season.'

She sat by the empty fireplace and tried to imagine his face and what he would have said. Then unbidden in the darkness another face appeared before her. *Marius King*!

Joanna shuddered involuntarily. She hadn't given

him much thought these last few weeks. But she bet that even now he would be following all the latest news about the new racing season. He would be especially interested in Hannibal . . . and her! Her mouth went dry with fear.

What had he said to her when he'd taken her hostage in the lift? That he would never forget how she had destroyed his world – *never*! And that his vengeance would be sweet. But now he was in prison, surely she was safe? How could he do anything to harm her from there?

Suddenly she was aware of a silver flame flashing before her eyes, burning away the image of Marius King to form two fiery silver eyes. Eyes she knew better than any others.

'XL?' she cried aloud. 'You're right, he will *never* beat us!' She jumped to her feet and made her way back over to the door. She was just about to turn the handle to let herself out when she heard voices coming up the corridor.

'I don't know what's got into Joanna these days,' she heard Agnes say. 'She's so moody and she's always disappearing off somewhere. I mean, where was she tonight for the egg turning?'

*I've missed the egg turning?* Joanna gasped. *I must have been in here longer than I thought.*

'I wouldn't take it personally, Agnes,' replied Mr

Hogan. 'She's obviously finding it difficult adjusting to the changes in the caves. I was wondering, does she have any interests outside the caves? What about friends?'

'She counts Excelsior as her best friend,' said Agnes. 'And of course she's very close to Marcia Chatfield, but she lives in Blackpool so they don't get to see each other very often.'

'Ah yes, the famous Mouse. I had to confiscate Joanna's phone the other day – rather too much texting and not enough maths!' came Mr Hogan's reply.

'I'd rather hoped she would get on with Isaac,' sighed Agnes.

'Give them time. I must say the boy has a natural ability when it comes to Latin . . .' The voices disappeared up the corridor unaware that on the other side of Vincent's door Joanna was standing there stunned.

*Friends? They think I haven't got any friends, except for Excelsior and Mouse. That's terrible . . . only they're right.*

She quickly let herself out of Vincent's study and hurried down to Excelsior's cave.

'Excelsior,' she sighed slipping down beside the silver dragon. 'Do you ever get . . . lonely?'

'Why should I be lonely?' said Excelsior. 'I see you every day.'

'But don't you miss Aurora?'

'I've never thought about it before,' mused Excelsior. 'I suppose of all the dragons I've ever met I like Aurora the best. I mean she's a Silver Spiked-Back, like me! Why do you ask? And why were you thinking about that horrid Marius King?'

'I didn't mean to think about him, it's just that I went into Vincent's study. I hadn't been there since . . . you know . . . last February and . . .'

'It reminded you.'

'Yes,' nodded Joanna, unconsciously resting her head against him. The familiar warmth and smoothness of Excelsior's scales immediately comforted her. 'Then I heard Agnes talking to Mr Hogan outside the door and she said that I was moody and didn't have any friends except for you and Mouse . . . And I hate the way everyone expects me to get on with Isaac!' Joanna glanced quickly over at the door, as if half-expecting him to be there.

'Actually, Isaac's really . . .'

'Don't you start, Excelsior! No, I need to make some new friends of my own.'

# 7
## AT HER MAJESTY'S
# PLEASURE

Marius King walked past the long line of tables and chairs already filled by his fellow inmates and sat heavily on the moulded plastic seat. More than anything it was the prison furniture that he despised. Of course he'd arranged matters to make himself more comfortable and he had soon established that he would not be sharing his cell however overcrowded the prison system became. Oh yes, he was already wielding his power. It never took him long to discover how to manipulate things to his own advantage. Almost immediately he had resumed a good many of his business interests, although the loss of the Brighton Caves was a terrible blow. He fingered with contempt the compulsory purchase order in his pocket that he had received from the WDRF five days earlier. Naturally he was challenging it in the courts.

In the meantime he had more immediate plans to put into action – like a small matter of revenge against the Brixton Caves! Marius King laughed out loud at the thought. Those nearby pretended not to hear but betrayed themselves by shifting nervously in their seats. Others stared straight ahead, unwilling to catch those ice-blue eyes staring back at them. Mr King had the perfect right to laugh at whatever he chose. It was certainly none of their business. Luckily he was distracted by the arrival of his visitor.

'You're late,' was the only welcome the visitor received.

'Sorry, Marius. Roadworks everywhere. How are you? Things are . . . ?'

'Tolerable, but I'd rather forget the niceties and get down to business. Tell me about the old woman.'

The visitor smiled. 'She was desperate to get her grandson started. She kept talking about the importance of passing on family trade secrets and why young people should dedicate themselves to the sport. You know the type – old school, loyal to a fault, honest, trustworthy . . .'

'Perfect!' smiled Marius King. 'And the boy? You think he'll co-operate when asked?'

'No question. He's so keen, he'll do anything, I'll guarantee it. He's nearly as obsessed about dragons as his grandmother. He'd be at the caves from morning till night, all day every day except he still has to go to school. And – you'll be delighted to know – Grandma's very keen that her grandson becomes good friends with little Ms Morris!'

'If it's not too beneath the *brat,* now that she's *World Champion!*' Marius King spat out the words viciously. 'Don't forget I want access not only to her and her dragon, but to Marlowe's study. Somewhere amongst his precious manuscripts is the secret of how to make that silver fire. If I'm going to destroy them, I need to learn all their secrets so they'll never race again.'

'It is my intention to personally oversee everything,' said the visitor with a smile.

'Make sure you do,' snapped Marius King.

'Marius, I *do* understand. Really, all you need to do is put your feet up and relax . . .'

'Sit and relax in this dump! How dare you! Surrounded by common criminals without an ounce of intelligence between them. As for the "screws" . . .' He turned a contemptuous glance at the prison guard standing over by the wall, who quickly looked away.

But the visitor's eyes flashed as furiously as Marius's own. 'Cut the temper and sulks with me, Marius. I know you too well. Remember you're stuck inside and if you want my continued co-operation, you'll have to show me a little more respect.'

Marius King scowled back. 'Don't forget that I

know enough about your past accomplishments to put you behind bars too!'

His visitor squirmed uneasily. Marius had obviously touched a raw nerve. Knowing he had gained the upper hand he continued.

'Sitting in the quietness of my cell has given me time to think – to develop my initial idea. Of course I want to exact revenge on the Brixton Caves but I'm sure you'll agree that to bring down just *one* cave seems rather insignificant. What I *really* want is something a little more spectacular, a little more ambitious. I want nothing less than to bring the world of dragon racing to its knees, to leave it reeling and gasping . . . ANNIHALTED!'

The visitor listened carefully, giving nothing away. 'Ambitious words, Marius. How do you intend to bring about this downfall?'

The prisoner's eyes gleamed brightly. 'By destroying all the dragons in this country. Every. Single. One!'

'No dragons, no WDRF – ingenious,' replied the visitor, interested at last by what was being said. 'Because if you *really* do want to destroy all the dragons, I know a very effective and relatively easy way that can be achieved . . .'

'I was hoping you'd say something like that!' said Marius.

'Of course it will cost . . .'

'With you involved, when has it not? But I want everything ready by New Year in order to wreak maximum havoc just as the major races of the season get under way.'

The visitor laughed out loud. 'Don't be ridiculous, Marius, I'll need to outsource this and find some research laboratory that needs funding for its own projects. It might take a little time to find one with the right level of expertise. And I'll have to cover our tracks. People do like to chatter so.'

Marius's face turned scarlet with rage. 'Chatter! If even a *whisper* of this is leaked to *anyone* . . . !'

The visitor showed no fear at what was left unsaid, although past experience showed the threat of violence was real – very real.

'Marius, you always were overdramatic. Have I ever let you down?'

Marius swiped the air with his hand as if swatting a fly. His irritation was growing by the second.

'For the present it looks like I am forced to leave everything in your capable hands. But I *want* a progress report *very* soon.'

The bell to mark the end of visiting rang shrill and sharp through the room. But before he was prepared to dismiss his visitor Marius had one final question.

'What have you told everyone about yourself? No one knows the connection between us, do they?'

'I just tell everyone that I've returned from abroad. It's a perfect cover!'

Marius King nodded his approval. 'Until next time then.' To his right and left came the sound of farewell sobs and muttered goodbyes, but Marius sat perfectly still in his chair and watched as his visitor disappeared through the door without a backward glance.

'Farewell,' called Marius after they'd gone, adding softly. 'Just as I intend to fare well.'

# 8

# PREPARATIONS

As the beginning of the season drew nearer, Joanna found (despite her lack of 'close friends') that she was very popular indeed. As World Champion all sorts of people wanted her to be here, there and everywhere – invitations that Spiky Mike dismissed by throwing in the bin.

'Why would anyone think that I'd allow Joanna to make a special guest appearance alongside some has-been celebrity who has nothing better to do than shop till they drop?'

However even Spiky Mike could not refuse one particular invitation that Agnes brought in after the end-of-morning lessons.

'Here you are, Joanna, this arrived earlier,' Agnes smiled. 'And not a special offer, ultimate experience or exclusive supermarket in sight!'

'Who's it from?' asked Joanna excitedly, as she took the thick embossed card from Agnes.

---

**THE WORLD DRAGON RACING FEDERATION**

**(GB DIVISION)**

**REQUEST THE PLEASURE OF**

**JOANNA 'JOJO' MORRIS AND THE**

**DRAGON EXCELSIOR**

**ON 5<sup>TH</sup> NOVEMBER**

**TO OPEN THE 75<sup>TH</sup> DRAGON RACING SEASON**

**WITH AN EXHIBITION DISPLAY**

**ON BLACKPOOL PROMENADE**

**AND TO BE GUESTS OF HONOUR**

**AT THE FOLLOWING RECEPTION**

---

Joanna immediately ran off to Spiky Mike's office. She knocked quickly and, hardly waiting for his 'come in', she burst inside and shoved the invitation into his hand.

'We are saying yes to this one, aren't we?'

Spiky Mike quickly read the invitation.

'About time too. I've been expecting this. I'd have been very annoyed if they'd asked anyone else to be guest of honour.'

'Really?' said Joanna.

Spiky Mike actually laughed. 'You're very modest for a World Champion. Not only are we going up to Blackpool to open the racing season, but as the week leading up to the race is your half term I've arranged that we stay with Frank for a few days.'

'Fantastic! I haven't seen Mouse in ages.' Joanna couldn't believe her ears. Spiky Mike had organised a treat for her!

'But it won't all be holiday. We'll have to run through the exhibition piece every day and of course your own races start the weekend after, so there'll be plenty of training too.'

'Training in Blackpool is always such fun,' replied Joanna. 'Excelsior loves flying over the sea, especially if it's really rough.'

'And you may be pleased to know that I accepted another invitation on your behalf. Earlier this morning Ms Lupin phoned asking if you'd like to take part in a fashion shoot. She wants to feature young flyers in the spring issue of *Dragon Fire* – as World Champion you'll be her star guest. She's going to ask Mouse and another young flyer, a novice this season called Dominic Pieterson, or "Cheetah" as he wants to be known.'

'Ms Lupin wants me to be in a fashion shoot?' exclaimed Joanna with delight, thinking of the glamorous fashion designer who made all the wonderful sequinned jackets worn by the dragon flyers. 'Did you *really* say yes?'

'I just said so. Why look so surprised? I'm not a complete philistine when it comes to fashion.'

Joanna had to stifle a giggle. Since Afra had gone up to Wales, Spiky Mike had returned to wearing his scruffiest T-shirts and jeans.

But having told her about the fashion shoot, Spiky Mike proceeded to ignore any further questions about when and where it would be.

'If you don't start concentrating on our exhibition piece I'll be phoning Ms Lupin to say you can't go,' he said, and from the tone of her trainer's voice Joanna knew it was not an idle threat.

Instantly she was all attention. 'We could fireball,' she suggested. 'That would impress people!'

'More like send all competitors fleeing back to their caves in fear wondering how they could even *think* of turning up for any race in which the pair of you were entered . . . but then . . .' Spiky Mike gave a little grin and whispered conspiratorially, '. . . then we'd have no secrets left for when it really mattered!'

They arrived in Blackpool in a howling gale. The wind was roaring in over the sea, whipping up the water into a cauldron of white fury that smashed over the storm defences of the promenade. Yet Joanna wasn't even looking at the sea as they drew up to the world-famous Blackpool Tower, home to Frank and Pat Chatfield's Blackpool Dragon Caves – she couldn't take her eyes off her friend, who was waiting for her at the entrance.

'Mouse! Is that really you?' Joanna asked in amazement. 'Your hair! You didn't tell me! When did you have it all cut off? And you've got *streaks*!'

'I wanted to surprise you. Don't you just love it!' exclaimed Mouse, styling it with her fingers. 'It's so much easier to have it short for my acrobatics.'

Joanna stared curiously at her friend. 'Are you wearing make-up as well?'

'I've been practising the eyeliner ever since I heard we're going to be fashion models! It was a bit fiddly at first, but I think I've got the hang of it now,' replied Mouse carefully examining the dark lines around her eyes in the reflection of the door. 'Come on in, I don't want the wind to mess up my hair.'

The two girls carried Joanna's suitcases up to Mouse's bedroom, which as Joanna had expected was plastered with posters of Hannibal.

'I put one on the ceiling last week, except I woke up to find it floating down on top of me. It gave me such a fright, I screamed,' exclaimed Mouse, flopping down on her bed. 'I don't suppose Ms Lupin has asked Hannibal to be in the fashion shoot too?'

Joanna laughed 'Apparently at nineteen, he's too old. He was mortified!'

'So what do you know about Dominic Pieterson?' asked Mouse. 'Did Spiky Mike say anything?'

'Only that he's a novice,' replied Joanna.

Mouse thought they needed to do some research so they looked up Dominic Pieterson's name on the WDRF website. Much to the girls' disappointment there was no photo but they discovered he was fourteen years old, had been born in the UK, and grown up in South Africa.

'Listen to this,' Mouse continued excitedly. 'It says here he was so inspired watching *Joanna Morris* become World Champion that he pestered his parents until they agreed to let him come to England to train with his grandmother, Carol McKenna, at the Suffolk Caves. A fan then, Jo! Wonder if he's good-looking?'

Joanna felt herself blush, but didn't say anything. She had been thinking exactly the same thing.

Mouse read on. 'Carol McKenna, who hasn't raced dragons competitively for the past three seasons due to ill health, is delighted that her grandson is carrying on the family tradition.'

'Does it say anywhere why he's called Cheetah?' asked Joanna, scrolling down the page. 'Perhaps it's a South African connection?'

'Hope it's not because he's going to be really fast!' Mouse looked almost worried.

Joanna scrolled down the page. 'All it says is: *Dominic was overwhelmed to discover that the dragons at his grandmother's caves had named him "Cheetah"*'

'I bet he *is* going to be fast then,' said Mouse glumly. 'I mean dragons just *know* these things, don't they?'

'Especially in your case!' laughed Joanna. 'I mean, you're *really* as quiet as a mouse, aren't you?'

It was so great being with Mouse again that it made Joanna realise more than ever how much she missed having a close friend in London. Her stay in Blackpool was just what she needed. Not only were there long chats with Mouse, there were no lessons with Mr Hogan, no Agnes to make her feel guilty and no Isaac snooping around Excelsior. She couldn't believe her luck when she also got rid of Spiky Mike!

On the second evening, Joanna had just settled Excelsior down in his cave when Spiky Mike had come hurrying in.

'Joanna, can I trust you to go through the exhibition routine and join in Frank's training sessions? I've just had a phone call from Afra. Hannibal is making his final preparations for the race and Aurora's having a few problems with her takeoff, so I said I'd go over to help sort it out.'

'Of course!' said Joanna trying to look concerned

rather than pleased that he was going.

Spiky Mike eyed her suspiciously, as if he'd guessed her true thoughts.

'I won't be back until the day before the race, so I'm trusting you to do everything Frank says – he'll be giving me a full report. And don't stay up all night gossiping with Mouse.'

The week flew by as quickly as Joanna and Excelsior skimming over the grey choppy waters of the Irish Sea. Without the pressure of a forthcoming race they were free to experience the exhilaration of speeding through wild gusts of wind, allowing themselves the thrill of cruising turbulent air currents that threw them perilously close to giant rogue waves that reached upwards as if to catch them.

'You're too good!' laughed Frank Chatfield in admiration. 'Perhaps you might have a word with Emilia about how to pull out of a dive without losing speed.'

'Of course,' said Joanna breathlessly, her cheeks glowing from the exhilaration of her flight. 'As long as you let Spiky Mike know how marvellous you think I am.'

Frank Chatfield laughed. 'I'll make an official announcement this evening when they all arrive from Wales.'

# 9
## THE
## CHEETAH

The next morning Joanna was up before anyone else. It was the start of the season at last! The Bonfire Novice Race. Could it be possible that this time last year she'd been one of the novice racers? It seemed like a lifetime ago. She wondered how Hannibal felt about having to fly in the race again. New rules from the WDRF stipulated that if *either* dragon *or* flyer were a novice, they had to take part in the race. Joanna had her own suspicions that the WDRF had only changed the rules because any appearance by Hannibal attracted lucrative advertising deals for them, such was his popularity. But Hannibal had just shrugged when he heard, saying it was a good test run for Aurora.

Joanna hurried down to the promenade, which was already crowded with workmen erecting marquees and stands and a series of flagpoles. Her heart gave a quiver of pride when she saw the black and gold flag of the Brixton Caves with its silver star flying from the central flagpole. She stood quietly, watching as it flapped in what was quite a cold breeze, until suddenly she felt a tap on her shoulder. Joanna turned to see a six-year-old girl staring up at her. She was wearing a replica outfit of Joanna's own racing gear, complete with a sequined dragon on the back of her jacket and sparkly gold trousers.

'Go on, Ruth, ask her,' said the girl's mother, adding, 'We've travelled over from Hull to see you in your exhibition. Ruth's a real fan you know. We were so delighted when you became World Champion.'

'Can I have your autograph?' The young girl had plucked up enough courage to thrust a pink velvet book towards Joanna.

'Of course!' said Joanna. Taking the girl's sparkly glitter pen she wrote:

'I hope you like it, it's my new signature. My friend Mouse taught me how to do it.'

Ruth looked suitably impressed. 'Look, Mum, it's just like a dragon.'

Any further conversation came to an abrupt halt as Spiky Mike came tearing up.

'I've been looking everywhere for you. Didn't you get my message about our meeting with Sir John Miller, the new WDRF president, to go through the arrangements for the afternoon?'

'I thought the meeting was at eleven,' said Joanna.

'It is . . . or rather *was*. It's ten past already.'

'Sorry, Ruth, got to go!' Joanna called hastily as she ran down the promenade after Spiky Mike. 'Hope you enjoy the exhibition!'

When Joanna shook the hand of the new WDRF president she found it hard not to giggle. Sir John was wearing a wig that had slipped precariously to one side. She could only watch in fascination as it threatened to fall off completely. The president seemed oblivious to the situation as he took out his clipboard and proceeded to read with great fervour, all the proceedings for the afternoon.

'Well, Joanna?' She suddenly felt a sharp elbow nudge from Spiky Mike. 'Sir John is asking if you have any questions. Have you?'

'Er, no thank you very much, Sir John.' She stood there smiling at him until she suddenly realised she was actually supposed to be taking some sort of action. 'So I'll . . .'

'Be getting changed, ready for the official photo?' prompted Spiky Mike.

'Yes, of course!' Joanna said, smiling again. 'Looking forward to it . . . umm . . .'

Spiky Mike took her by the arm. 'Come along, Champion.' Then he hissed, 'Did you hear a single word of that? No, I thought not!'

Safely out of the way of the WDRF president Joanna finally exploded with giggles. 'I couldn't help it! It was just his . . .'

'Wig? Yes, I saw it too. He's not exactly the classiest president the WDRF has ever had!'

By contrast, the opening exhibition by World Champion Joanna 'JoJo' Morris and her dragon Excelsior was pure class. Full of spirals and swoops, all performed at top speed, it left no one in any doubt that they were issuing the challenge: *We are the champions. Beat us if you dare! Beat us if you can!*

They landed to thunderous applause and a storm of flashes and camera clicks.

'Stay with me to watch the race,' said Excelsior unexpectedly.

'Of course!' agreed Joanna immediately. 'I didn't fancy watching it from the VIP stand at all. Though it'll be strange watching and not racing, don't you think? I wonder if Aurora's nervous?'

Joanna looked down at the golden sands to where the dragons and their flyers were making their preparations. Hannibal had drawn a middle lane and was standing by Aurora's side waiting for the siren to mount and begin the mind-blend. Joanna ran her eyes along the row of waiting dragons and gave a gasp.

'Look, XL! Look at that huge golden dragon at the end on the right. I don't even know what it is.'

'It's a Golden Chimera,' said Excelsior. 'We've never raced one. I think they're supposed to be fast, but not very agile. Where's his flyer?'

Suddenly they saw a figure running across the sand. Joanna couldn't see his face, but emblazoned across the back of his jacket was an enormous snarling golden cheetah.

'Oh!' said Joanna, her curiosity ablaze. 'That must be Dominic Pieterson. I wonder what his dragon's name is?'

She took out her programme.

'You were right, the dragon *is* a Golden Chimera and it goes by the name of Nemesis.'

Any further information had to wait as the siren to start the mind-blend sounded. Immediately the spectators fell silent, their eyes trained on the contestants down by the water's edge. As the flyers prepared to race Joanna automatically found herself intoning the mind-blend questions too. Immediately

Excelsior answered and before they knew it they were watching the race in a deep mind-blend and with it came all their own racing instincts.

The contest began with a great flurry of dragon wings furiously beating the air. From all around the spectators roared into life. Hannibal's fan club was out in strength and a high-pitched wail repeated tirelessly, *$H_2O$ Go! Go! Go!* Like them, Joanna's eyes were fixed on the Brixton team as she willed them into the lead.

'Keep it steady, Aurora . . . watch your speed now while you level out . . . and fly . . .'

Yes! Aurora's sleek silver body seemed to move effortlessly ahead of the tangle of dragons.

'Brilliant start,' admired Joanna.

'Lucky to have escaped that collision,' added Excelsior. Joanna looked over to where two dragons had collided in racing for the same patch of sky. One of the dragons was large and gold. It had to be Nemesis! Cheetah ploughed on, regardless that the other dragon had to almost stop in mid-flight to change direction. Joanna was rather shocked if not a little impressed at his single-mindedness. Once he had flown clear, Joanna turned her attention back to watching Hannibal and Aurora. They had a substantial lead which was growing all the time and Joanna relaxed into enjoying the race.

'Ms Morris!' the loudness and abruptness of

the voice forced Joanna to suddenly snap out of the mind-blend. She felt Excelsior shudder at the unexpectedness of it. Joanna turned to see Sir John scowling at her imperiously. Immediately she felt a wave of anger. He should have known better than to forcibly cause her to break a mind-blend. Somehow she managed to stop herself saying something rude.

'Ms Morris, did you not understand? The instructions for the timetable today require your presence in the VIP stand so that you are ready to award the winning medals at precisely the correct moment.'

'Sorry,' said Joanna, 'but my dragon asked me to watch the race with him and I want . . .' She broke off suddenly. From every side, shrieks and wails rose from hordes of hysterical girls, and all along the promenade people were pointing at the big screens. What had she missed by talking to that stupid president? Something dreadful must have happened at the 180-degree turn that marked the halfway point of the race!

'JoJo, LOOK!' called Excelsior, who hadn't taken his eyes off the race for one second.

'What?' said Joanna, frantically trying to find the screen that showed the replays of dramatic moments in the race. When she saw it, she gasped.

Hannibal and Aurora had made the halfway turn, only to find the great gold Chimera flying directly towards them. It was only Hannibal's racing experience that saved them. He forced Aurora into a sudden dive to avoid a head-on collision, but they'd dipped so suddenly that neither Hannibal nor Aurora had the chance to register a huge wave that broke over the pair of them. It looked like they were going to end up in the sea. Somehow Hannibal steadied Aurora and slowly, slowly managed to take her out of danger from any other maverick waves – or dragons. Unfortunately the Golden Chimera was now in the lead.

'You can't do that!' protested Joanna immediately to Sir John. 'That must be Deliberate Obstruction.'

'I think you'll find,' corrected Sir John, 'that both flyers are equally responsible for positioning, see Rule 7, section ii, paragraph 5. Now, we really must return to the VIP stand.'

With great reluctance, Joanna left Excelsior and followed the president. The screens told the story. Aurora trailed behind Nemesis all the way to the finishing line; in fact Hannibal nearly lost his second place to a rather good Polish flyer, Bartek Szeptunowska, who put on a quick spurt at the end.

As the dragons landed on the beach, Joanna hoped and prayed that the flag announcing a stewards' inquiry would go up. But none appeared.

She looked over to the winners' enclosure. It was impossible to see the winning dragon or its flyer through the surrounding throng of photographers.

It was so unfair. She was going to have to present the medal to this boy when he really didn't deserve it. Joanna looked over to where Hannibal was waiting with Aurora. Both he and Afra were more involved in checking over Aurora's wings than bothering about anything else. She badly wanted to go over to them, but the tannoy was announcing: 'Ladies and gentlemen the presentation of the winners' medals and sash of the 123rd Bonfire Novice Race will be made by the World Champion, Joanna "JoJo" Morris.'

The president thrust a ribbon and medal into Joanna's hands and pushed her towards the winners' enclosure. Joanna found herself included in yet another storm of camera flashes as she reluctantly walked forward to present the medal.

Dominic Pieterson was standing by his golden dragon and smiling. Smiling at Joanna, smiling at *her* . . . smiling . . .

And he was gorgeous!

Joanna's heart skipped a beat. Could her heart really skip a beat? She felt her cheeks burn red and somehow she managed to put the medal over his head. He had to bend down so that she could reach and her hand somehow touched his hair. Did she really touch his hair? It was like a black curtain sweeping across his face and when he brushed it back to reveal dark green eyes and long black lashes . . .

Joanna felt her legs go wobbly and her mouth was dry, although somehow she managed to say, 'Congratulations!'

'Thanks!' he smiled at her again. He looked down at the medal. 'I never expected to win in a million years! Is Hannibal OK? They gave us such a surprise appearing like that, I didn't really know what to do. The way Hannibal manoeuvred Aurora out of the wave was brilliant. I can't believe I've beaten him and won my first race.' His voice had a faint South African accent.

'Just like I did last year,' Joanna found herself agreeing as she gazed up into those gorgeous green eyes. 'It's a great feeling, isn't it?'

'Ms Morris?' interrupted Sir John.

Joanna turned round snapping, 'What? I'm just talking to the winner.'

'You need to make the presentations to the second and third places!' insisted the president.

Joanna was rather pleased to see Dominic trying to suppress a grin. But as she caught sight of Hannibal still checking over Aurora, she suddenly felt guilty.

'Yes, of course, I'm coming now.' She turned back to say goodbye to Dominic 'Cheetah' Pieterson, but already the paparazzi were swarming forward.

Joanna hurried over to give Hannibal his medal. 'Is Aurora OK?'

'We'd have been fine if that *idiot* had kept his dragon under control. Chimeras may be notoriously difficult to manoeuvre but he flew that one like a block of wood. Welcome back to novice land, I suppose. He didn't have a clue what to do so I had to choose between crashing into him or taking a dip in the sea. I knew it would cost me the race.'

Joanna nodded and smiled as best she could. She knew Hannibal was right, but – she hardly dare admit it even to herself – she couldn't help be glad that Dominic had won.

'Aurora was amazing! Kept a cool head the whole time,' Hannibal continued, proudly stroking the long silver neck of his dragon. 'At least next time we'll be competing against someone who knows how to fly.'

'Who's that?' said Joanna absentmindedly. She couldn't stop thinking about those green eyes.

'You, kid,' laughed Hannibal. 'Better start practising a bit harder now. Oh, but first I think you'd better go and give Bartek his third-place medal before he passes out in anticipation!'

# 10
## RACING
# AT LAST!

'Our turn!' sighed Excelsior contentedly, as they arrived at the racecourse for their first race of the season. 'Last week in Blackpool I could hardly stand it as all those dragons took off over the sea. I could feel my wings quivering in anticipation.'

'You think you had it hard,' said Joanna. 'At least you didn't have to go round with President Sir John "I've got my list". While I had to do all that medal presenting I saw you enjoying having your photo taken with all those fans.'

'Surprised you noticed!' remarked Excelsior slyly. 'Because you didn't enjoy meeting a certain young flyer at all, did you?'

'I . . .' Joanna knew her cheeks were blushing bright red. The trouble with mind-blending was that it was impossible to have any secrets from her dragon.

'Hurry up and check all the screens to see if he's racing this afternoon!' continued Excelsior. 'I know you want to – shame about his dragon though – who ever thought of the name Nemesis? Plank or Bulldozer would be much more suitable.'

'Look over there, isn't that Chris Perry on Tom Tom,' said Joanna trying to change the subject. 'They must be over from Australia. And there's that new flyer Bartek Szeptunowska on that rather fierce-looking Black Sabre dragon, Prince Krakow. As long as we don't have to start next to them. I don't want those nasty fangs anywhere near me.'

'Oh Krakow's great! He wouldn't hurt a fly,' said Excelsior enthusiastically. 'I was chatting to him after the Novice Race. He has so many amazing stories to tell. Apparently his mother laid him during an electric storm . . .'

But Joanna was spared further details as Spiky Mike arrived to tell them it was time to go to the starting line.

The first race was an easy quick sprint along the top of the Sussex Downs in the golden sun of late autumn. Joanna and Excelsior left their fellow competitors far behind.

'Well, that was a breeze,' sighed Excelsior, as they landed in pole position. However, Spiky Mike was on hand as ever to throw cold water on their triumph.

'That was a sloppy takeoff – don't let me see it again.'

Fortunately for Joanna, before he could make any more disagreeable comments, he was commandeered by a sports reporter.

'Is he always such a hard taskmaster? I thought your takeoff was brilliant. Is this Excelsior? I didn't get the chance to see him last week.' Dominic Pieterson suddenly appeared from out of nowhere.

Joanna's heart gave a little leap. She'd recognised his voice immediately.

'Hello,' she tried to say as normally as possible, which was quite hard as she could hear Excelsior whispering, '*Ooh look, it's the Cheetah!*'

'Are you racing?' she added hastily.

'Yes, the final one.'

'Oh!' said Joanna, blushing madly. 'Me too. I didn't see your name on the board.' Would he guess that she'd looked?

'I'm a late entry because I won the Novice Race.'

'Aren't you going to introduce us, JoJo?' Excelsior nudged Joanna and let out a snort of smoke.

'Give me a chance, XL! Dominic, this is Excelsior.'

'Hi, Excelsior, you beauty!' He turned back to Joanna. 'I've seen so many photos of him but he's even more amazing in real life.' Joanna could hear the genuine admiration in his voice.

'Dominic!' A woman in the crowd called his name.

Dominic groaned. 'That's my nan! She gets worried if she doesn't know where I am for five minutes. But I can't complain because it's thanks to her that I've got to fly. She was the one who persuaded my mum and dad to let me train. When you became World Champion she insisted that the time had come!'

It wasn't just one woman who appeared but two.

'Carol McKenna, pleased to meet you, my dear,' the older woman dressed in tweeds and wellies suddenly clutched Joanna by the hand and promptly shook it. 'What an inspiration. And now here you are making friends with my grandson, Dominic . . .'

'Nan!' protested Dominic.

The second woman added, 'The Brixton Caves are the team to watch, Dominic. Both Joanna here and Hannibal Henry Oliver have a very good technique. I follow with keen interest everything that goes on in all the other caves – especially the work of Joanna's trainer, Spiky Mike Hill.'

Joanna turned to look at her. She looked like her voice – careful and controlled, with her dark hair carefully styled in a sleek bob. She was wearing expensive-looking black trousers and matching jacket.

'We haven't been introduced. I'm Dr Trix Dawson, Dominic's trainer.' The woman held out a leather-gloved hand.

As Joanna returned the handshake she felt the trainer's eyes watching her carefully. It made her feel slightly uncomfortable so she was rather relieved when Dominic's nan distracted Trix Dawson by calling out, 'Oh look, the lanes for the final race have just gone up.'

They all turned to study the board. Joanna's first instinct was to look for where Hannibal was in comparison to her. She had drawn pole position in the centre. Hannibal was three to her left and . . .

'Look, Dominic,' his nan sighed with satisfaction. 'You're next to Joanna.'

'Oh!' replied Dominic. 'That's a bit nerve-racking. I'll see you at the start then, Joanna.'

Joanna couldn't help grin. 'Yes, I'll see you there – and Dominic, it's Jo, my friends call me Jo.'

'Oh, heck!' grimaced Excelsior, as they watched Dominic Pieterson follow his trainer. 'Not next to the Plank! Right, it'll be a takeoff that Spiky Mike will talk of for years to come! Sorry, JoJo, I don't care if you think Dominic Pieterson is the best thing since sliced bread but I'm not hanging around Demolition Duo a second longer than I have to.'

Of course it wasn't Nemesis they really had to worry about. As Joanna and Excelsior settled into the mind-blend, all their concentration centred on the small square of clear sky directly ahead of them, they knew without doubt that the same space was equally coveted by another Silver Spiked-Back dragon and her flyer only a few metres away.

At the starting siren Excelsior's sleek and powerful body exploded skyward like a bullet. For one brief moment Joanna felt slightly sorry for Dominic and Nemesis as they left them standing on the starting line. However all such thoughts soon disappeared. Hannibal and Aurora had got off to a brilliant start as well.

The two silver dragons flashed across the sky like parallel streaks of lightning. They zigzagged across each other's paths trying to find any thermals that might give that extra advantage of speed. As they approached the halfway point – Chanctonbury Ring, a circle of beech trees planted on the remains of an Iron Age fort – Joanna looked across to check their position. A thrill of exhilaration rushed through her. They were neck and neck. This was what both teams had been waiting for – a real race! Hannibal was starting to manoeuvre Aurora into the best position to make the turn by circling around the trees in the tightest arc he could and Joanna was about to jockey for position when suddenly Excelsior asked, 'How brave are you feeling?'

'What are you planning?' asked Joanna, although she'd guessed already, sensing Excelsior starting to spin his fire. 'OK, I'm up for it!'

Joanna opened her mind to the great wall of spinning fire inside Excelsior. She was riding the crest of the wave . . . then through into the stillness as Excelsior spun on the spot and she was out on the other side of the fire wave. There was no stopping them now as they headed towards the finish line leaving a stunned Hannibal chasing after, wondering what he had just witnessed.

'AWESOME! That was awesome!' Hannibal leapt off Aurora's back, and came rushing into the winners' enclosure. 'How did you do it?'

Joanna didn't get the chance to reply. She could hear from the boos of the crowd that the flag announcing a stewards' inquiry had been raised.

'Not because we fireballed surely?' groaned Joanna.

'We'll soon find out!' replied Excelsior. 'Here comes the president.'

Sure enough, Sir John was scurrying along, rule book in his hand. He came to a sudden halt as Spiky Mike stepped in front of him.

'Show me! Just show me it's illegal! No? You can't, can you? Because I've already checked. It says nothing, absolutely nothing about it.'

Sir John waved the rule book at Spiky Mike. 'Just because something is not written in here does not mean the action was legal. I would suspect it was covered by Section 17, point 3a: Irregular Behaviour During a Race.'

'Nonsense, man – it was sheer brilliance!' interrupted Hannibal. 'I'm not complaining.'

'Come on, award the race to Jo and XL,' insisted Spiky Mike.

But the president refused to withdraw his objection and by default the race was awarded to Hannibal, who in turn refused to accept it. A third place Chris Perry on Tom Tom was eventually persuaded to accept the victory.

'So that was a successful day for the Brixton Caves!' announced Spiky Mike as they all climbed into the van to drive back home.

'Shut up, Mike, your sarcasm is more than I can stand,' snapped Afra uncharacteristically. 'Just drive.'

'OK! OK!' said Spiky Mike. 'But I've already had it up to here with the president's rule book.'

'And I'm fed up with hearing about your run-ins with the powers that be. Just shut up and drive.'

Joanna looked across at Afra, completely shocked. Her dark pretty face was tight and pinched, all her features lost in a deep scowl. She'd never seen her like this before. She was more than upset – she was furious. Did she secretly agree with the Sir John . . . or was she jealous?

*What a strange day it has turned out to be*, thought Joanna as they pulled out into the road. Then, looking out of the window she gave a little smile – at least it was ending very satisfactorily. Standing at the exit to the racecourse, waving at her, was Dominic Pieterson.

# II
## GO, JO!
## GO, JO!

Agnes was worried. The racing season had only just started and already there was open disagreement in the Brixton Caves. Spiky Mike was ranting and raving in his office, while Afra was coldly silent down in Aurora's cave. Neither was speaking to the other. Agnes was sure that the problem was not *really* about fireballing itself, although the WDRF hadn't helped matters by descending on the caves the day after the race to discuss the issue.

Spiky Mike was supposedly filling in the ten-page form that the WDRF had insisted on if he wished to apply for 'official' recognition of fireballing, so Agnes made her way down to Aurora's cave. Afra didn't look up from grooming the dragon.

'Hannibal's not here – he's got some interview with an American magazine up in town.'

'It was you I wanted to see,' said Agnes.

'I'm a bit busy at the moment.'

Agnes looked across at Afra. She had turned her back towards the old woman and Agnes suspected she was close to tears. Agnes stood there waiting patiently.

Finally Afra sighed. 'He always wins! Whatever *I* do it doesn't matter, *he* always does something better. The race – it was neck and neck between the pair of them, first Aurora then Excelsior. Hannibal and Joanna knew it too – just pure speed and skill – and then . . . then that stupid fireballing and Hannibal and Aurora didn't stand a chance. I know! I know! It's a race and Joanna and Excelsior wanted to win just as much as Aurora and Hannibal. It's just . . . why can't it all be simple?'

Afra turned and looked straight at Agnes. 'Do I sound like a bad loser? It's not really the losing – our first race against them meant that was always on the cards – what hurt the most was that Mike hadn't even told me about the fireballing. Not even a whisper.'

Afra put the brush she had been using back into the tackle bag that hung on the cave wall.

'What did he say after the race?' asked Agnes.

'He said he didn't know they were going to try the fireballing in the race. But that still doesn't excuse the fact that he hadn't told me.'

'And what would you have done if he had?'

'I don't know, Agnes. I just don't know. The funny thing is Hannibal doesn't seem to mind at all. He just thinks the fireballing was amazing. Says we were beaten fair and square!'

Agnes didn't say a word.

'You think I'm in the wrong, don't you?' Afra shook her head furiously and wiped her eyes quickly on her handkerchief. 'Why not just say it? I'm jealous, plain and simple. See, I've said it. The thing is, I haven't the faintest idea what to do about it!'

'Just do what you do best,' said Agnes. 'Train your flyer and your dragon. Goodness we're only at the beginning of the season. And talk to Spiky Mike – tell him how he made you feel and then set ground rules you can both agree to.'

Afra nodded. 'It just brought back last year. When I trained Prometheus, Marius King was always going behind my back.'

'I don't think your boyfriend has sunk that low yet,' said Agnes with a smile. 'Although from the sounds coming from his office as he attempts to fill in that WDRF form I may be wrong.'

'What do you mean the WDRF won't decide on fireballing until their next full council meeting? And has anyone asked the dragons?' protested Excelsior one week later, when Spiky Mike finally received news of his application. 'Perhaps it's time we had some official dragon representation. I could start a Dragon Union. And I want to make sure that it's noted that I discovered fireballing!'

'OK! OK! I get the message,' said Spiky Mike. 'Believe me, I'm just as annoyed as you are but there's nothing else we can do. I'm beginning to wish you'd never discovered fireballing, the amount of trouble it's giving me.'

He smiled sheepishly at Afra, who had just entered the cave and returned his smile. They had obviously made up with each other.

'Mike, Ms Lupin is on the phone. She says she'd like a quick word with you about a convenient date for this fashion shoot with Joanna and Dominic Pieterson.'

'Ooh, the *Cheetah*!' hissed Excelsior in Joanna's ear as Spiky Mike stepped outside the cave to take the call.

'Shut it, XL.' Joanna glared at her dragon. Already she could feel the familiar red glow that spread across her cheeks every time anyone mentioned Dominic's name. She looked away but too late, Afra had noticed.

'Dominic Pieterson?' she started to say with a questioning smile, before noticing Joanna's look of utter embarrassment. She quickly changed direction. 'I wonder what you'll get to wear?'

The fashion shoot was eventually timetabled for the Saturday before Christmas, but Joanna was hoping she'd see Dominic Pieterson sooner than that – preferably at the qualifying heats for the first big race of the season, the New Year Derby, which took place in the second week in December. Much to their relief, as top seeds Joanna and Hannibal had been entered in two different heats since only the winner of each race was certain of qualifying.

The morning of the heats Joanna got up extra early to wash her hair. She stared hard at herself in the mirror and frowned. She might be thirteen, but the two plaits she wore for racing made her look like a ten-year-old schoolgirl!

*Perhaps I should get Afra to braid it for me like hers, or should I cut it short like Mouse? I loved her streaks.* But she knew her mum would never let her colour her hair like her friend. She did however wear the lip-gloss that Mouse had sent her as she couldn't be there in person to support her. According to her friend it would make her lips look *irresistibly* gorgeous and shiny. She popped the tube into her jacket pocket to touch it up before (and after) the race.

Once at the racecourse Joanna got changed so

quickly that she ended up having to stroll around all by herself while she waited for the other flyers to come out. Autograph hunters appeared from every direction and Joanna found herself swamped by a horde of fans. She squiggled her dragon name at least fifty times, desperately trying to see through the crowd of fans who, being younger than Joanna, had come with an equal number of tall chaperoning parents.

Finally she was free to look round. Most of the flyers were out now. There was Chris P, Lady Danielle Campbell-Lee and Bartek with the long Polish surname. Hannibal was *very* busy talking to a new flyer, Niamh McGrath, who was obviously enjoying the attention, but where was Dominic?

'He must be here,' she said to herself, trying to beat down the pang of disappointment. 'Perhaps he's running late.' She scoured the race boards for his name three times before it dawned on her that as winner of the Bonfire Novice Race he was guaranteed a place in the New Year Derby. She made her way over to Excelsior feeling rather deflated.

'Oh what a shame, Cheetah's not here then,' said Excelsior rather too cheerfully for Joanna, but on seeing her crestfallen face he added, 'I was just thinking about takeoff.'

They watched Hannibal and Aurora demolish any

competitors in the first heat. Joanna had to admit their takeoff was very impressive, as was their finish. So did Spiky Mike. He came hurtling over to Joanna as she waited in the pre-race enclosure.

'Did you see their time – close to the track record? It will give them pole position in the New Year Derby. I want that place.'

'Right, like he has to tell *us*!' Joanna fumed as she walked by Excelsior's side to the start point.

'I'm ready when you are,' agreed Excelsior. 'I've a score of my own to settle with the WDRF president for disqualifying us last time.'

As the flyers climbed onto their dragons and settled themselves down to prepare for the mind-blend a hush fell on the spectators. But Joanna had already forgotten the crowds as she leant her face against Excelsior's. As soon as the first siren sounded she softly began to intone:

*What are you?*
*I am a dragon?*
*What is your name?*
*My name is Excelsior*
*What type of –*

Suddenly a sound shattered her concentration. 'Go, Jo! GO, JO! G-O-O!'

Joanna looked around in confusion as a flurry of dragon wings rippled all around her. The race had started and she and Excelsior were still on the ground. Her face blazed red with embarrassment. She knew without looking who'd called out. That accent was instantly recognisable. Dominic Pieterson was here after all!

She flung herself back into the questions, but Excelsior did not immediately answer.

'I'm sorry, XL . . .'

'Do you want to race or not!' snapped Excelsior. Joanna stared in astonishment. Excelsior was never cross.

'I . . .'

'Come on, mind-blend!'

Joanna quickly ran through the mind-blend questions, constantly aware how the seconds and flying dragons were speeding away and then she was at the final question:

*Shall we mind-blend?*

Excelsior barely waited for the order to fly as he ripped through the air, chasing after the racing dragons.

Once within the mind-blend all Excelsior's angry thoughts came flooding into her own. 'Dominic Pieterson might be lousy at takeoff but he has no right to inflict that lack of ability on us!'

'How was I to know he would call out like that? Look, I'm sorry. Let's think about pole position . . .'

'Pole position? We'll be lucky to qualify!' came Excelsior's cold reply.

'XL, I really didn't know he was there, I . . .'

'Doesn't matter,' said Excelsior. 'It's just that we're going to have to pull out all the stops now. Are you ready?'

Then without warning Excelsior began to curl the fire in his belly, Joanna gasped in amazement. 'But we'll be disqualified if we fireball.'

'But I'm not *spinning* the fire,' exclaimed Excelsior. 'I'm *curling*!'

Joanna suddenly understood. Of course – curl, not spin! Deep within the mind-blend she knew exactly what to do. Just like a surfer in the waves she could ride the curl of fire. As she opened her mind to slip down the crest of flame the exhilaration of pure speed flooded through her. They were flying faster than they'd ever flown before and it was wonderful!

They left the rest of the field in their wake and as they came into land Excelsior had to seize the muddy ground beneath him with his claws to avoid crashing into the nearest spectator stand. Joanna leapt off Excelsior's back, laughing hysterically, as she threw her arms around her dragon's neck.

'Wow that was amazing! Let's always fly like that!'

'I could throttle the pair of you!' exclaimed Spiky Mike, as Joanna flashed the gold medal at him. 'At this rate I'll be grey by the end of the season. And don't think that just because you won I'm not going to ask you what on earth happened at the beginning of the race.'

'I was distracted by . . .' Joanna felt her cheeks blaze red. 'A spectator.'

'What! You were distracted by a spectator?'

'So? I got pole position!'

Fortunately, before he could say anything else, Hannibal and Afra came over to the winners' enclosure to congratulate Joanna.

'Hey, why the cross faces?' said Hannibal. 'That was an awesome piece of flying. No wonder that Dominic Pieterson is so starstruck by you, Jo! Shame he can't keep his big mouth shut when he knows flyers need to concentrate.'

To Joanna's embarrassment she saw Afra elbow Hannibal and silently mouth, *Don't say anything*. Hannibal took one look at Joanna's bright-red face and a grin suddenly crossed his face.

'Sorry, Jo – didn't realise.'

'Think I'm going to get changed now,' said Joanna hastily, hurrying away before anyone could make any more comments.

Spiky Mike turned to look at his girlfriend in

dismay. 'Oh don't tell me that novice Dominic Pieterson has got a thing about Joanna. That's all I need – one lovesick teenager sabotaging my flyer!'

'Mike, you really are slow at times,' laughed Afra. 'I think you'll find it's not one lovesick teenager – but two!'

# 12
## THIS IS
# NOT A GAME

Marius King did not like being in prison. However he did not intend it to inconvenience him any more than was necessary. A small "chat" with the prison governor who believed in taking time to get to know the inmates proved *very* productive. How fortunate to discover the governor had fourteen-year-old twin daughters besotted with a certain Hannibal Henry Oliver!

'Ah, Hannibal! Such a talented flyer. I remember going to the States to watch him fly for the first time.' Marius smiled across the table at the governor as if he were some minor employee. 'Would you like me to arrange a signed photograph for each of the girls?'

The governor was delighted. 'Could you really? They'd be over the moon.'

'Their names?' asked Marius, pretending to take

a biro from his pocket only to express regret that of course he didn't have one. The governor promptly gave Marius his own gold fountain pen. Marius started to write, then promptly put the pen down.

'Actually, one quick phone call and I can have the photos here by this evening. May I?' He pointed at the governor's phone.

'Be my guest,' said the governor.

The outcome of the meeting – as Marius had hoped – was an invitation to watch the racing with the governor in his office. And when Marius arranged some memorabilia for the girls (some old racing gloves and some sequins from Hannibal's original Brighton jacket) the governor could hardly refuse Marius's request to meet his visitors in the privacy of his office. Marius was content for the time being with the privilege.

However, on a certain December afternoon all such feelings were swallowed up in the blinding rage that consumed him as he watched the *brat* and her dragon decimate all competition. As he watched them fly over the finishing line his hatred boiled over. He snatched up the phone and roared down the receiver, 'Here! Thirty minutes!'

He turned to the stunned governor.

'I want full use of this office – and no guard. Failure on your part will result in the newspapers hearing of my *gifts* to your daughters.'

The governor turned pale and stammered, 'Of course, Marius . . . anything you say.'

'It's *Mr King*,' snarled Marius angrily. 'Now get out!'

Marius's temper had not abated by the time his visitor arrived.

'My patience is beginning to wear thin. You saw the race today. How much humiliation do I have to bear by seeing the Brixton Caves triumph again and again? I want action and I want it now!' He banged his fist down onto the table.

'Temper, Marius!' His visitor was decidedly cool. 'Apologise or I won't tell you the good news.'

Marius continued to scowl angrily, but the visitor was determined to make him sweat just a little longer.

'No apology? Oh dear we *are* in a bad mood. How about three guesses as to my news, Marius?'

'Three *guesses*?' Marius King's voice snarled under his breath. 'Let me remind you this is not a game.'

Something in his tone of voice told his visitor that this had gone far enough. Time for the announcement.

'Dragon Influenza!'

*Dragon Influenza*. Marius King repeated the words over to himself and suddenly smiled, his anger completely forgotten as the potential of those two words began to dawn on him.

'Tell me more.'

'I have found a laboratory that has manipulated the bird flu virus HN51 into a new flu virus HN23/7 – all in the name of researching a vaccine for the human population of course. For a great deal of money I obtained a batch of this new virus. Oh, Marius you'll love this – the virus, completely harmless to humans, extinguishes a dragon's fire.'

'Its very life breath!' Marius King laughed softly to himself. 'I really couldn't ask for anything better.' He looked sternly across the table at his companion. 'And don't forget – I want everything ready by the New Year.'

'That's impossible . . .' the visitor began to say, but Marius interrupted them impatiently.

'You have the virus, so why the delay?'

His visitor smiled. 'I thought why not have a bit of fun with the WDRF, dangle a lifeline by offering them a cure. I can guarantee that the WDRF will be so desperate that we'll be able to name our price. Wouldn't it be fun to extract an extreme amount of money from them?'

'*You* can make as much money as you like,' hissed Marius King, 'but just remember that *I* want to be sure the whole of the dragon-racing world has come tumbling down around me first!'

'I understand, Marius.'

'So when will everything be ready?'

'It will probably be more like February. But I *do* want you to be assured that everything is progressing well.'

'February!' Marius King spat out the word angrily, but his visitor was not intimidated by his outburst. 'You're just going to have be patient, Marius. Of course if you'd prefer someone else to be helping you in your current situation I will gladly withdraw . . .'

Marius King suddenly laughed. 'That won't be necessary. You must excuse my temper today. Sometimes I get let's just say *a little frustrated* at my current abode – something that I am working on. Just remember, I do not easily forgive those who betray me!'

'Betrayal, Marius? How could you say that after all I've done for you?' His visitor looked genuinely hurt, but Marius King ignored the comment and instead glanced quickly up at the clock on the wall.

'Do you have any more news for me?'

'You'll be pleased to know the grandson is being extremely co-operative about getting to know Joanna Morris and I'm hoping soon to have full access to the *entire* Brixton Caves.'

Marius King was suddenly all attention. 'Including Marlowe's study?'

'Should be just a few weeks . . . perhaps days.'

'A few weeks . . . days even and Marlowe's secrets will be mine . . .' Marius King leant back in his chair and repeated the information over slowly to himself. By the time he looked up his visitor had gone.

# 13

## SPRING DAZE

'Hannibal has been teasing me about Dominic all morning . . . he's worse than my brother,' exclaimed Joanna bursting into Excelsior's cave. She stopped. Excelsior wasn't alone. Crouched down behind him was Isaac! He quickly stood up.

'Sorry, Joanna, I was just examining Excelsior's claws. He did ask me,' he added hastily, seeing the look of horror on Joanna's face. 'I've finished now. Hope you enjoy your fashion shoot tomorrow.'

Isaac quickly left the cave. Did Joanna see him wink at Excelsior or was she just imagining it? She knew he didn't have a terribly high opinion of Dominic. She'd overheard him talking to Hannibal about the collision in the Novice Race and neither of them had a good word to say.

She turned quickly to Excelsior. 'Please tell me I

didn't say anything too embarrassing in front of Isaac. I'm beginning to wish tomorrow was over already.'

'Who cares what other people think?' said Excelsior. 'And anyway, I bet Ms Lupin's got everything organised and it will be great. Didn't you say Mouse was coming down too? She's sure to have been practising fancy poses in front of the mirror.'

Joanna laughed. 'Yeah, Mouse is great. She's never bothered about what people think of her. I mean she goes up to Hannibal and *tells* him to sign her T-shirt – and he does! I'm sure I'd never have the courage to do something like that. So what will you get up to tomorrow, XL?'

Excelsior gave a little cough. 'Actually I will be undergoing a beauty treatment of my own. Isaac and Spiky Mike are filing my claws. Ever since our last race they've been very uncomfortable. That landing was not one of my best.'

'You don't mind that I'm not here, do you?' said Joanna, looking with concern at his claws.

'I'll survive!' said Excelsior in mock exaggeration. 'And so will you!'

'Ooh! Jo, come and see Ms Lupin's Christmas tree!' exclaimed Mouse, dragging Joanna through the glass doors of the exclusive Mayfair fashion house as soon as she arrived early the next morning. 'It's pale pink with tiny white lights and it's gorgeous, and you'll never guess what . . .'

But Joanna didn't get a chance to guess because just then Ms Lotty Lupin, owner of Lupin Designs, appeared. She smiled to see the two girls looking so excited.

'We're just waiting for Dominic and then we'll go up to the studio and I'll explain how the day is timetabled.'

'Can I just show Jo your Christmas tree first, Ms Lupin?' said Mouse. 'It's *so* gorgeous!'

Mouse took Joanna over to the Christmas display where Joanna had to admit the tree was very pretty, although she said that she liked real ones the best.

'So do I,' said a voice behind them. 'It's the smell, isn't it? It just says "Christmas".'

Joanna kept her eyes firmly on the pink Christmas tree, already aware that her cheeks were a far deeper shade than the tree. What if she kept on blushing all though the photo shoot? Aware of Mouse grinning at her from ear to ear, she took a deep breath and turning to face *him* she beamed, 'Hello, Dominic. Meet my best friend Marcia Chatfield.'

'Everyone calls me Mouse,' said Mouse looking at Dominic with great interest. Joanna was rescued from Mouse's questioning eyebrows by Ms Lupin calling them upstairs.

The studio was a hive of activity. There seemed to be a bewildering army of make-up artists, hairdressers, lighting assistants, personal assistants . . . but as soon as Ms Lupin entered the room they all fell silent and turned towards her, waiting for the order to begin.

'Good morning, everyone!' said Ms Lupin. 'Before we start I'd like to introduce our models for today – Mouse Chatfield, Dominic Pieterson and . . .' Ms Lupin turned with a smile to Joanna. '. . . our star guest, our very own World Champion, Joanna Morris.'

A ripple of applause ran round the room, so Joanna gave an embarrassed wave.

'Let's get to work,' said Ms Lupin with a smile.

Immediately the studio buzzed into life. Joanna found there was no time for shyness or embarrassment as Ms Lupin's assistants set to work with make-up and brushes, clips and hairspray There was also a glorious array of jackets and trousers, footwear, headwear and a whole treasure chest of accessories that made up Ms Lupin's Spring Daze Collection, all in bright acid greens, pinks and yellows. By the time they had finished, Joanna hardly recognised the girl staring back at her from the enormous mirror.

'Do hurry up, Jo!' called Mouse, her voice quivering with excitement. 'I'm desperate to see you.' As Joanna flung back the dressing-room curtain she heard Mouse give a huge whoop of delight.

'I wish we could look like this every day!' said Joanna, unable to take her eyes away from their reflections. 'We look *so cool*!'

The two girls made their way back to the studio to find it had been transformed into a great green garden in the middle of which was a huge fake tree.

'Hey, Jo, up here,' called Dominic dangling his legs over the branch to reveal a dazzling pair of lime-green trousers. 'Come on up. It's an easy climb.'

'Hold it right there!' Out of nowhere a man with a very sophisticated and expensive-looking camera appeared and snapped Joanna staring up in astonishment at Dominic.

'Great shot,' he murmured. 'Carry on!'

'Perfect!' called Ms Lupin. 'That's just what I want you to do. Play around in the garden and our photographer will snap away.'

They spent the whole morning swinging on the branches, playing chase, hide and seek, and doing all sorts of acrobatics. Mouse even taught them both how to do a cartwheel until, exhausted, Joanna lay down under the tree.

'Joanna, close your eyes and don't move!' The photographer snatched another camera from the table. 'Lotty, cut the lights except for those three at the side. And take out the pink filter and put in a blue one. Great, now turn on the lights in the tree.'

The studio had fallen silent except for the *click*, *click* of the camera. Joanna desperately wanted to open her eyes. *What was going on? Why had Mouse suddenly stood up and tiptoed away? Where was Dominic?*

'Open your eyes, Joanna.' The photographer's voice sounded very close.

And there was Dominic staring down at her from the tree all covered in sparkling lights. He swept his dark hair out of his eyes and smiled such a wonderful smile, that all Joanna could do was smile right back.

*Click.*

'And thank you very much, everybody!' called Ms Lupin. 'Lunch time. We'll start back at one-thirty.'

The lights snapped back on, but Joanna continued to lie there dazed.

'Wake up, Jo!' said Mouse, waving her hand in front of her eyes, pulling her friend up and gently guiding her in the direction of the changing rooms. 'So he's gorgeous. Would it help if I said I think he likes you too?'

'How long are you in town for?' Mouse asked Dominic, aware that as Joanna was incapable of asking even the simplest of questions, she'd better help her out. Joanna managed a grateful smile at her friend.

'Just the weekend—' he suddenly stopped and

turned to Joanna. 'Actually, Jo, I haven't any plans for tomorrow, so I was wondering if I could come and see the Brixton Caves. That's if you're not busy?'

'The Brixton Caves?' Joanna desperately wanted to say yes, but she and Mouse had planned to go Christmas shopping weeks ago. Now what should she do? She looked across the table at Mouse, who turned away and started to crunch an enormous apple.

'OK,' said Joanna. 'How about eleven o'clock at the town hall steps?'

Dominic looked so pleased and had so many questions to ask that suddenly Joanna found it the easiest thing in the world to sit there chatting about the caves. She didn't notice that Mouse had disappeared until Ms Lupin asked where she was, when it was time to get ready for the afternoon session.

Joanna found her friend down by the pink Christmas tree. Mouse ignored her and went and stood by the lift doors,

'Mouse, what's the matter?' Joanna pulled her friend round to face her.

'Nothing!' Mouse wiped her eyes quickly with a tissue. 'I don't want to stop you showing Dominic the caves. It's just that . . .' she blew her nose hard. 'I've been looking forward to our shopping trip for ages.'

Joanna looked at her friend horror-struck.

'When you didn't say anything upstairs I didn't

think you minded. Don't you know you're my best friend ever? Of course I'll come shopping with you tomorrow.'

'Really?' said Mouse, her face brightening already. 'Yes, really!' exclaimed Joanna, linking arms with her.

The afternoon was a resounding success. They had to pose in tight-fitting metallic jackets and leggings around gigantic replicas of gold and silver dragons.

'I can't wait to see the photographs,' said Joanna as they sat in the reception area waiting to go home.

'Can we do it another time, Ms Lupin?' asked Mouse eagerly. 'It was such fun.'

'Yeah, it's been brilliant!' agreed Dominic. 'And great to escape Nan and my trainer! Oh, great, here they come, right on cue. Well, bye, Mouse, nice to meet you. I'll see you at five tomorrow, Jo. Enjoy your shopping.'

Mouse turned to Joanna with a surprised look on her face.

'You don't mind, do you?' said Joanna anxiously. 'Your train back to Blackpool goes at four so that gives me loads of time to get to the caves by five. Just in time to see Excelsior being fed and then I can take Dominic to watch the egg turning.'

'What? And show him off in front of Isaac?' laughed Mouse. 'I wish I was there to see that.'

'Well,' said Joanna, 'it's important for Isaac to realise that we don't necessarily share the same opinion of Dominic Pieterson.'

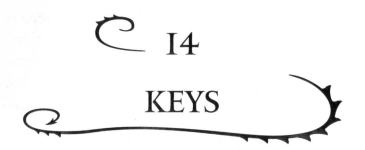

# 14

# KEYS

The clock tower was just striking five as Joanna hurried across the road to where Dominic was leaning against the wall of the town hall waiting for her.

'Hi, Jo, did you have a good day shopping with Mouse?'

Joanna found it impossible to look him in the face without blushing so she concentrated on all her bags of shopping and talked very fast.

'Yeah, we had a great time, and I got my presents sorted out, which is quite a relief because I know Spiky Mike is intent on practising tomorrow even though it's Christmas Eve.'

'Nan says he's the best trainer in the business,' said Dominic.

'He is,' agreed Joanna. 'And the most difficult to please. You've seen how he likes everything to be perfect – except his desk, which is like a rubbish dump. I'll show you.'

Joanna had already decided she would impress Dominic by using the front entrance to the caves. She only used it herself on special occasions as it was quicker to use the back way. They went through a door marked 'Private' and along a short passage until they came to a lift. She couldn't help but feel a wave of pride as the lift doors slid open to reveal panels of finely wrought gold metalwork showing flying dragons. The lift descended quickly and they stepped out into the circular entrance hall with its creamy silk walls covered with huge golden-framed oil paintings of dragons and most spectacular of all – Joanna's favourite – a huge crystal chandelier suspended from a flying dragon.

'Welcome to the Brixton Dragon Caves!' She smiled with satisfaction as she heard the gasp of surprise that she'd just *known* Dominic would make. Joanna led Dominic through a pair of doors into a wide and very long corridor lined with brightly lit glass cabinets, from which shone countless awards and cups. She stopped in front of two enormous trophies.

'And these belong to me and Excelsior! Well, at least until the summer.'

'The WDRF Speed Record Shield and the World

Championship Cup – amazing!' Dominic was genuinely impressed. 'I never imagined them so big!'

'Do you want to hold them?' asked Joanna 'Wait there and I'll go and get the key from Agnes's office.' She soon returned with a small bunch of keys and unlocked the glass cabinet. 'Can you lift it down? I'm not quite tall enough.'

Dominic carefully took out the great silver cup and, holding it aloft, solemnly declared in a very good imitation of Sir John Miller, 'The winner of the WDRF World Championship Speed Race is . . .'

He waited for Joanna to stand to attention.

'Dominic "the Cheetah" Pieterson on his Golden Chimera, Nemesis!' He paraded up and down the corridor with the cup held high in the air, before carefully putting the trophy back with a half a smile. 'That's probably as close as I'll get to ever doing that. I mean when will I ever beat *you?* Which was best, breaking the speed record or becoming World Champion?'

Joanna looked thoughtful. 'Excelsior really wanted to break the speed record, but I . . . I wanted to be World Champion, not just for me but for Vincent.'

'He was the owner of theses caves wasn't he? And he died . . .'

'He died saving me. He was the best. I still miss him so much . . .'

Joanna quickly locked the cabinet and put the keys in her pocket. 'Come on, let's go and see Excelsior. He'll be wondering why I haven't been to visit him today. At least I have Mouse's Christmas present for him!'

Even now Joanna felt a thrill whenever she entered Excelsior's cave. He was never quite as she remembered him – somehow more real, more dangerous, more *dragony*!

'Hey, XL,' she cried throwing her arms around him. 'Yesterday was so fab – I can't wait to see the photographs – and then today Mouse and I went Christmas shopping and look!' Joanna waved a pink tissue-wrapped present in front of Excelsior. 'It's from Mouse, but she says you have to wait till Christmas! And you have a visitor.'

'Ah, Dominic Pieterson, the Cheetah,' murmured Excelsior to Joanna so only she could hear. 'No wonder you seem so happy!'

Dominic stepped closer to Excelsior and gave a nod. 'Great cave you've got.'

Before Excelsior could reply they heard another voice calling down the corridor.

'Joanna, is that you?'

'Ah, Isaac!' said Joanna, rolling her eyes. 'On cue as usual!'

'It *is* my supper time!' insisted Excelsior. 'You don't

want me wasting away now.'

Isaac poked his head around the door. 'I thought I heard you. What are you doing here on Sunday evening? Is everything OK?'

'Of course!' replied Joanna crossly. Who did Isaac think he was questioning *her* about being at the caves, acting like *he* owned them and not her.

'I've brought my friend Dominic to see the caves,' she said pointing at Dominic, who was looking with great interest at the oil lamps on the wall. 'He's the flyer—'

'Oh, yes, the Cheetah – who beat Hannibal in the Novice Race!' Isaac nodded a brief greeting before disappearing out of the cave. 'Back in a minute, XL.'

Joanna stared after him, furious. Was he trying to provoke her? Why did he make Dominic's name sound like an insult! And since when had he started calling Excelsior 'XL' – that was *her* name for her dragon!

She turned towards Excelsior.

'I didn't say he could!' insisted Excelsior quickly, reading her mind. 'He's just winding you up, JoJo. Anyway, he did a brilliant job on my claws, they don't hurt a bit now, so don't be too cross.'

When Isaac returned with Excelsior's supper Joanna was torn between snatching the bucket from his hands and sticking out her foot so that he tripped up. Before she could do either, Isaac turned to her and said, 'Feed him if you like. I've got a plenty of jobs to be getting on with.'

'Thank you,' said Joanna coldly, taking the bucket from him. 'And by the way, Isaac, my *friend* Dominic and I are coming to watch the egg turning.'

Isaac shrugged. 'Fine. Just don't be late. You can leave Excelsior's bucket, I'll clean it after.'

Dominic couldn't help but smile as Isaac disappeared through the door.

'Not a close friend then. Still you're lucky having someone like Isaac to do all the grotty jobs like feeding and cleaning up. How come he's your Egg Turner?'

'His grandma's *really* our Egg Turner. He's just a trainee. Oh drat, I forgot, I've still got Agnes's keys, Isaac will need them if he wants to get into the Nursery Caves.'

Joanna ran after Isaac but when she reached the ancient wooden doors that led to the Nursery Caves she stopped in her tracks, too shocked to move. The doors were open. That could only mean one thing: Isaac had his own set of keys when *she* didn't! She stormed down the passageway to where Isaac was preparing for the egg turning.

'How come *you've* got keys to the Nursery Caves?' she shouted, unable to control the feelings of anger that swept over her.

Isaac turned round quickly, looking shocked at Joanna's explosion.

'I've got so many jobs to do. They gave me a set just to make life easy . . . they told me not to tell you.'

Joanna could hardly believe what he was telling her. *They?* Did he mean the Trustees or his grandma? Or who? Joanna was so angry and so hurt she couldn't speak. She turned on her heels and walked out.

# 15
## STUDIES IN
## THE LIBRARY

Joanna was still fuming by the time she got back to Excelsior's cave. She flung the bunch of keys across the floor.

'Isaac doesn't need *these*! Apparently *he* has his *own* set!'

'JoJo, they're just keys!' said Excelsior trying to calm her down.

'Are you all right, Jo?' Dominic sounded very concerned.

The sound of his voice brought Joanna up sharply. She'd been so upset she'd forgotten he was there. She let out a sigh. 'Isaac has keys to the Nursery Caves.'

'And that's a problem because . . . ?' asked Dominic.

'They're *my* caves, and I haven't. He was told not to tell me.'

'That doesn't seem fair,' agreed Dominic sympathetically. 'Look, I don't need to see the egg turning, but I'd love to see the rest of the place.'

Joanna immediately flashed him a grateful smile.

'Show me where these go,' Dominic picked up the keys, 'and I'll put them back for you.'

First Joanna took Dominic to visit Aurora in the neighbouring cave, then they went to the training cave, then the loading bay where they kept the transport vans and finally the office shared by Spiky Mike and Afra.

'Guess which is Spiky Mike's desk?' laughed Joanna pointing first at an immaculate desk with a diary, telephone and laptop all carefully positioned and then at the adjacent one covered in piles of untidy letters, circulars and dirty coffee mugs.

'Now you know the truth about my trainer! So where next, Agnes's office or the library?'

'Could we go to Vincent's study?' asked Dominic hopefully. 'I mean, wasn't he a scientist with lots of equipment for experiments and things?'

Joanna shook her head.

'Sorry,' she said quietly. 'I can't. It still hurts too much. Perhaps another time.'

'That's OK,' said Dominic. He went and picked up one of the dirty mugs. 'How about we wash these up and put you in Spiky Mike's good books.'

Joanna couldn't help but laugh.

'OK, washing up, and then how about the library? That's where I do my lessons.'

'You're *so* lucky not to go to school,' said Dominic enviously. 'I do, and every time I'm in a race I have to go and ask the headmaster to take time off!'

The washing up took considerably longer than expected, partly due to the fact they kept finding dirty mugs and partly because they decided to have a cup of tea themselves. Eventually they made their way down to the library. Joanna pushed open the doors with a flourish then stopped. For the second time that evening she was frozen with surprise.

Isaac was adjusting the angle of a reading lamp, and sitting beside him thumbing through the pages of an old book of manuscripts was Mr Hogan. What was he doing there? It was obvious that the pair of them were so intent upon their studies that they hadn't noticed her. And then it dawned on Joanna what they were doing – or rather *attempting* to do. They had sneaked into Vincent's study and taken one of Vincent's books on alchemy.

'What's going on?' she heard Dominic whisper behind her.

Suddenly Joanna found her voice and stormed into the library. 'That book is *mine*! Mine! How dare you steal it!' She had never been so furious in all her life.

As Isaac looked up at her a mixture of emotions swept over his face; shock, guilt, but also boldness.

'I didn't know you were still here . . .' was all he managed to say.

Mr Hogan swung his chair around to face Joanna, but he spoke first to Dominic.

'Young man, would you mind waiting outside, I need to speak to Joanna in private.'

'Stay, Dominic!' ordered Joanna, her voice trembling. 'You are *my* guest in *my* caves. And I want you to stay.'

'Jo, I think it would be better if I wait outside, I'll go and look at the trophy cabinet again.' Dominic closed the doors behind him.

'I really don't understand why you are making such a fuss, Joanna,' exclaimed Mr Hogan. 'Vincent would have want—'

'How do you know what Vincent would have wanted?' exploded Joanna. 'You never even met him. And if it's so fine to be studying them, why are you both slinking about when you think no one else is around. Why not just get it out in lesson time? That stuff belongs to me and *no one* is going to use it without my permission. Put it back NOW!'

'Mr Hogan, let's put it back. We should have asked,' said Isaac resignedly as he closed the book shut. But Mr Hogan was not so ready to admit defeat.

'I want you to reconsider, Joanna. Knowledge such as this,' he tapped the cover of the book, 'should not, *must* not, be withheld from anyone who wishes to learn. I'm *certain* Vincent would approve.'

'Mr Hogan,' Joanna's voice was just above a whisper. 'Don't try and tell me how important Vincent's work was – it saved Hannibal's life and it saved mine. *When* I am ready I will allow Vincent's things to be made available. BUT NOT TO PEOPLE WHO STEAL IN LIKE THIEVES.'

'Joanna, I am your teacher! How dare you speak to me like that!' Mr Hogan looked genuinely shocked.

He wheeled his chair over to Joanna. Now, instead of angry, he looked strangely vulnerable, even sad.

'I can see you're upset, it's just you don't understand quite how vital these manuscripts really are. I beg you to reconsider.'

When Joanna refused to even look at him, Mr Hogan turned back to Isaac, who was sitting at the table tracing the design on the book cover with a finger.

'There's nothing more we can do now, take the book back to Mr Marlowe's study, Isaac.' As Mr Hogan followed Isaac out of the library he stopped in the doorway. 'I might as well tell you now, Joanna, as soon as the holidays are over I will be speaking to the Trustees about not only using Vincent's books, but also his scientific equipment.'

'You can speak all you like,' said Joanna defiantly. 'You're not having Vincent's stuff unless I say so!'

Joanna found Dominic pretending to be engrossed by the old photos next to the trophy cabinet.

'I think I've found a photo with my nan in.' Still looking at the photograph, he added quietly, 'Are you OK, Jo? I'm sorry if my being here has made things difficult for you. It's probably time for me to go – you look worn out.'

'I am!' admitted Joanna. 'But I'm glad you came. Come on, I'll take you out the front way.'

Back on the town hall steps Joanna suddenly felt shy again as she came to say goodbye.

'Have a good Christmas, Dominic, and I'll see you at the New Year Derby.'

Dominic gave a wave and was about to go when he suddenly put his hand in his pocket. 'Nearly forgot to give your keys back! Sorry, I wasn't quite sure what to do with them.'

Joanna took the keys and watched as he disappeared down the road. Dominic was so nice. At least *he* understood her.

# 16
## SEASON OF
# GOODWILL?

'And a Merry Christmas to you too, Ms Morris. Seems you get what you want every time.' Isaac stood in the entrance to Excelsior's cave. 'Don't mind if I come in, do you?'

He walked into the cave before Joanna had the chance to reply, and began stroking Excelsior's smooth silver scales.

'Hey, boy,' he muttered. 'I won't be seeing as much of you as usual. I'm taking a break . . . Just came to say goodbye.'

'What?' Joanna dropped her copy of *Dragon Racing Today.* Isaac's dark face, usually all smiles, was ashen.

'Oh, don't pretend that you care, Joanna Morris. You've wanted to get rid of me ever since I started training as an Egg Turner. And now you've got your wish – I messed up big time last night!'

Joanna was stunned to see Isaac shudder visibly. 'You'll have to feed Excelsior yourself now, but you won't mind that, will you? Have a nice life, Joanna! Mine's ruined!' Isaac slammed through the cave doors and let them bang shut behind him.

'Go after him, JoJo,' Excelsior shoved her towards the door. But Joanna just stood there.

'I don't think I'm the person to talk to him at the moment.'

As soon as Joanna thought a reasonable amount of time had gone by, she went to find out what had happened. Afra was the only one around and told her everything.

'When Agnes came in this morning she noticed that yesterday evening's entry for the egg turning hadn't been filled in. She went down to the Nursery Caves to check things and saw that the dial on the box was turned to 'Off'. The egg was barely warm. She's down in the caves now with Mike, trying to save it. She's terribly upset and blaming herself saying she gave Isaac too much responsibility too soon.'

'Oh!' said Joanna. A million and one emotions were whirring round her brain. Was this *her* fault because she'd shouted at Isaac? Perhaps she'd momentarily distracted him at the vital moment? On the other hand it wasn't the sort of thing that happened by accident. What if he'd done it deliberately in a fit of temper just to spite her? She felt a flare of anger. She was certainly *not* going to feel sorry for him.

'Is he coming back?' asked Joanna.

'He's gone home for now but Mike's left the decision up to Agnes. I think she's going to think about it over Christmas and will make up her mind early in the New Year.'

When Agnes finally appeared with Spiky Mike, her face was set with a grim sad frown.

'The egg is fine. If you'll excuse me I must fill in the egg-turning diary.' She walked slowly up the passage and disappeared into her office, shutting the door firmly behind her. Joanna could hardly bear to watch and in a rush of remorse blurted out to Spiky Mike, 'I think this might be my fault.'

'What makes you say that?' asked Spiky Mike.

Joanna explained the fiasco of the previous evening.

'Your behaviour was unbelievably childish, but that doesn't excuse the fact that Isaac made a disastrous mistake for which he has to take responsibility. As for the incident with Mr Hogan, I think you know it's something we will need to discuss.'

Joanna started to protest, but Spiky Mike stopped her. 'In the *future*. Now instead of making any more fuss or trouble, go and feed your dragon . . . and wash up afterwards!'

'What a horrid Christmas this is going to be, XL! Poor Agnes. What on earth made Isaac turn down that dial?' Joanna was frantically scrubbing out Excelsior's food trough.

The dragon didn't reply immediately, but then he said a very curious thing:

'Do you really think it was Isaac? I mean he's meticulous in everything he does.'

'Who else could it be?'

Before Excelsior could comment further there was a knock and Hannibal stuck his head round the cave door.

'I just popped in to say goodbye before I go and pick up my parents from the airport. I'm supposed to be showing them a traditional UK Christmas. Now I feel bad about taking a few days vacation and leaving everybody with the extra work. What was Isaac thinking? Poor kid, he must be devastated.'

'It's quite a mistake!' exclaimed Joanna.

'Yeah, but we all make mistakes. Mine nearly cost me my life.' Hannibal looked at Joanna knowing that she too was remembering his previous dragon, Prometheus.

'Isaac should be given a second chance,' said Hannibal. 'I'd trust him any day with caring for Aurora.' He took a tiny package out of his pocket. 'Before I go, here's your Christmas present, Jo.

You can open it now if you like.'

'See!' piped up Excelsior, 'Some people know you don't have to wait for Christmas Day to open your presents.'

Joanna hardly heard him for she had unwrapped Hannibal's gift . . . a brooch of a cheetah!

'Merry Christmas, Jo,' called Hannibal already disappearing down the corridor.

Joanna ran after him to thank him when she suddenly saw the door to Vincent's study was wide open. None of the lights were on. Who could possibly be in there? It was too dark to see anything but Joanna thought she could hear muffled breathing. Was someone hiding there? Perhaps Isaac had sneaked in to *borrow* a book as an act of defiance before he went home. She felt along the wall for the light switch and turned it on.

'Got you!' she cried, half expecting to catch Isaac red-handed.

What she saw was far more terrible.

'No!' She let out a loud cry and ran straight to where Agnes lay in a collapsed heap next to the fireplace.

'Agnes! Agnes!' Joanna desperately patted her face. Agnes groaned and fluttered her eyes. Joanna let out a deep breath. At least she was conscious!

'Help me . . .' Agnes's voice was little more than a whisper.

'Yes, of course, oh, Agnes . . .' Joanna stood up, her legs were trembling but she managed to run to Spiky Mike's office and burst in breathlessly. 'Quick, Agnes is ill!'

Spiky Mike leapt to his feet and was out of the office in a flash.

'Where is she?'

'In Vincent's study,' called Joanna running after him.

Spiky Mike took one look at Agnes and took out his mobile to call 999. Joanna was amazed he could be so calm as he told her to first go and get Afra, who was down with Aurora, and then to go and wait at the entrance for the ambulance so she could bring the paramedics down when they arrived.

Joanna looked at Agnes through a haze of tears. She seemed so frail and helpless on the floor.

'Will she be OK?' Joanna managed to stutter.

Spiky Mike looked up. His apparent calm was belied by a face pale with shock and worry.

'I don't know,' he said shaking his head softly from side to side. He picked up Agnes's hand and rubbed it gently. 'I just don't know.'

# 17
## TRYING TO
## MAKE SENSE

Isaac kicked off his trainers and threw himself down onto his bed.

'Stupid, stupid idiot!' For the fiftieth time he went through the events of the evening before, trying to find the point where he'd made the terrible mistake.

He'd gone down to the Nursery Caves about 5.25 to start his preparations for the egg turning . . .

Isaac got up off his bed and pretended he was in the Nursery Caves going through his routine.

'OK, so then I put the fireproof gloves ready on the shelf and I was just getting the tongs from the hook.' He pretended to take down the tongs. 'And that was when Joanna burst into the cave and started shouting at me about the keys.'

He grimaced. He'd always known she'd make a fuss about him having keys.

'So then Joanna stormed out and I . . . ?' That was the trouble – he couldn't remember what he'd done next. He'd been so upset by what Joanna had said that he'd decided to turn the egg straightaway in case she should come back with her new pal, Dominic Pieterson, and make more trouble. He'd turned the egg and closed the lid just as he always did.

Had he been in such a hurry or so upset that somehow he'd knocked the dial? But how? And to forget to fill in the egg-turning diary – what had he been thinking? He knew the answer to *that* question only too well.

On coming out of the Nursery Caves he'd seen Mr Hogan coming out of Vincent's study with a large book of manuscripts. Mr Hogan was having a little trouble manoeuvring his wheelchair so he'd gone to help. Then he'd got caught up in the excitement of trying to translate some of the Latin text – until Joanna had burst in on that too. Of course she had every right to be upset *that* time. They shouldn't have taken the book from Vincent's study without clearing it with the Trustees first.

*Don't suppose it makes any difference now. I've blown everything so completely that I'll be lucky if they let me anywhere near the caves*, thought Isaac bitterly. He picked up an already-opened Christmas present from his bedside table.

*Well, Hannibal, so much for your Christmas gift!* He thumbed through the pages of a new and very large Latin dictionary and threw it down carelessly. *Because I won't be needing it now.*

Isaac turned off the light and lay back down on his bed. It was like being in some dreadful nightmare from which he couldn't wake. He couldn't bear the thought of not turning the egg again. He could see it in his mind's eye. At first glance the egg looked a pale yellowy gold with small silver speckles, but Isaac had soon discovered that there were small deep golden markings crisscrossing the shell. They were more marked and darker at the narrow end of the egg. And recently he'd noticed the egg was getting heavier. In the spring, just a few months from now, he would have felt the first movements of the dragon inside its shell . . .

'Isaac! Isaac!' His mother's shocked voice snapped him out of his reverie at the same time as the snap of the light switch broke the darkness.

'Mum? What's the matter?' He jumped up off the bed, screwing up his eyes at the bright light. His mum was crying.

'It's Grandma! She's been rushed to hospital with a suspected heart attack. I'm going up there now.'

Isaac could only stare aghast at his mother.

'Grandma . . . a heart attack . . . is she . . . can I come too?' Isaac rushed to put on his trainers but found his fingers were shaking so much he couldn't tie the laces.

'Please, Isaac, I need you to stay here. I can't get hold of your brothers, they'll be home soon. Dad's just back and he's going to take me. I'll call you when I have any news.'

'Give Grandma my love,' Isaac called after his mother, who was already halfway down the stairs. Things were going from bad to worse. He sank back down onto his bed. 'Grandma, don't die!' he sobbed. 'Please don't die! Oh, it's all my fault! If I hadn't messed up the egg turning, you wouldn't have got upset . . .'

*Except . . .*

Sitting there alone in his bedroom Isaac was suddenly completely sure that he had not turned down the dial on the box.

But if it hadn't been him, then who?

That Sunday evening there had only been himself, Mr Hogan, Joanna and that Cheetah boy in the caves. It didn't make any sense. He certainly remembered locking the door behind him. But whoever had done it didn't need *his* keys; there was a full set of keys for the caves hanging up in his grandma's office. Everyone was always borrowing them. In fact, Joanna must have been using them to show Dominic Pieterson around.

*But Joanna would never do anything to harm the dragon's egg no matter how much she dislikes me.*

*And I was with Mr Hogan from the minute I came out of the nursery cave to when we both left to go home. So that leaves . . . Dominic!*

Isaac's train of thought was interrupted by a loud knock at the front door. He ran down to open it. His brothers were always forgetting their keys. But when he opened the door he saw to his astonishment that it wasn't any of his brothers – it was his friend Aaron Morris. And standing just behind him . . . his sister.

'What d'you want?' he said blankly, looking past Aaron and straight at Joanna.

She'd obviously been crying too, but Isaac felt too numb to care. 'I said, what do you want?'

'I'm really sorry about your grandma—' Joanna started.

'If you've just come to tell me that you can go,' snapped Isaac.

'No, I—'

'Hurry up, Jo,' her brother urged her. 'Mum said to be quick.'

Joanna took a deep breath and said, 'Isaac, please will you come back and turn the egg?'

Isaac stared at Joanna. Had he heard her properly? A whole raft of different emotions swept over him – relief, happiness, anger – and the knowledge that they couldn't manage without him. Part of him wanted to hurt Joanna, just as she'd hurt him. Wouldn't it serve her right if he refused? But he quickly pushed those thoughts away. He couldn't do that however mean Joanna was to him. It must have cost her to come to his house to ask. Standing here she could barely look at him.

'Please, Isaac.' She was begging him now. 'If you don't, the dragon inside will die. Do it for Agnes and for the egg . . .'

'Of course I'll do it,' he said, not looking at Joanna either. 'Now if you don't mind, I'm waiting for my brothers to come home.'

'Come on, Jo, you got what you came for.' Aaron pushed his sister back along the path, and turned back to his friend. 'Hope your gran's OK, mate.'

Isaac closed the door and let out a huge sigh. 'Just get better, Grandma!' he whispered. 'And then I'll show you just how proud of me you really can be.'

# 18
## A *HAPPY*
# NEW YEAR?

'Agnes is going to be in hospital for some time yet while they run tests,' said Spiky Mike addressing everyone at the first meeting after the Christmas break. 'But the doctors are very pleased with how she is responding to treatment. I went to see her yesterday and she wishes everyone good luck in the New Year Derby with the expectation of seeing the cup in the trophy cabinet when she returns. Which brings me to my next point. Isaac, on behalf of all the Trustees I'd like to thank you for continuing to egg turn under what must have been very difficult circumstances. However now that the initial crisis is over, and on your grandma's advice . . .' Spiky Mike hesitated.

*Come on, spit it out*, thought Isaac.

'You must be supervised by either Afra or myself.'

Something in Isaac suddenly snapped. 'You all still think I turned down the dial. The thing is . . . I didn't!'

'But you were the last one in the Nursery Caves on

Sunday evening, Isaac,' Afra said softly.

'I know I did not touch that dial,' insisted Isaac. 'I think someone went in after me and changed it.'

Joanna leapt to her feet. 'Are you accusing me?'

'No, not you,' said Isaac.

'I certainly didn't do it!' exclaimed Mr Hogan.

'I know that too,' said Isaac.

'Are you saying it was *Dominic*?' Joanna jumped to her feet again. 'But that's ridiculous. He was with me all the time and we didn't go to the Nursery Caves.' She turned to Spiky Mike for support and was delighted to get it.

'That's a very serious accusation, Isaac, for which you have no proof. I'm sorry, but for now you have to be supervised, and if you don't like it then I'll have to hire an Egg Turner from the WDRF.'

Isaac nodded knowing he had no choice. 'Fine. Supervise me then.'

Spiky Mike looked relieved and started discussing travel arrangements for the New Year Derby.

Joanna barely heard him, she was so furious with Isaac for accusing Dominic. Everyone could see how ridiculous it was when he'd been with her all the time.

Except he hadn't! He'd waited outside the library whilst she'd had that row with Isaac and Mr Hogan. Suddenly she turned really cold. Dominic had picked up the keys when she'd thrown them on the floor . . .

No, she was being ridiculous. How could someone who didn't know his way around go anywhere near the Nursery Caves? He wouldn't have had time and . . .

No, it was too ridiculous to even consider it. She forced herself instead to concentrate on what Spiky Mike was saying.

~~~

Tensions were high as they set off for the New Year Derby. There would only be one winning team that afternoon.

*This is the race where Hannibal beat Joanna last season,* thought Afra as she and Spiky Mike led the dragons down to the pre-race enclosure. Could Aurora beat Excelsior?

Afra looked to where her boyfriend was settling Excelsior. She watched half in pride and half in envy. Spiky Mike had a second sense when it came to dragons.

*But not teenage girls,* thought Afra. Spiky Mike might be Joanna's trainer, but *she* was always the one Joanna came to for help. Afra turned back to settling Aurora. She really was the sleekest, most elegant dragon Afra had ever seen, never wasting any energy by unnecessary movement. Hannibal seemed content flying her, almost protective of her. What worried Afra was the niggling thought that Hannibal still missed Prometheus. Had he been so infatuated by the power of the creature that it had left a gap that could never be filled?

'Please win,' she sighed to herself as Hannibal appeared out of the changing rooms to the accompaniment of screams and shouts from his adoring fans. If a race could be won on popularity, then Hannibal would win hands down.

Afra started to walk over to Hannibal to give him his final racing brief when suddenly she heard a shout. She looked up to see Joanna calling her from a nearby dressing room window.

'Afra! Help, my zip's stuck on my jacket. Quick, before anyone sees.'

As Afra rescued Joanna's zip she couldn't help but smile. Joanna had obviously just applied some lip-gloss, only it had smudged.

'Jo,' she whispered, 'before you go, give your chin a wipe.'

By the time Joanna finally emerged from the changing rooms the enclosure was busy with flyers, some just chatting, others signing autographs. Joanna noticed a huge crowd of girls around Hannibal and went over to stand by Excelsior.

'I don't mind if you want to go and socialise with the other flyers,' said Excelsior.

'I'm quite happy thank you, XL,' said Joanna, rather

too quickly. She pretended to read her programme but anyone watching closely could see that Joanna kept looking over to the male changing rooms.

'I don't think he's come out yet,' said Excelsior, matter of factly.

'Why should I care?' replied Joanna.

The truth was that Joanna wasn't sure that she wanted to see Dominic. What if Isaac had told the truth and Dominic *had* turned down the heat for the egg? There! She'd admitted it as a possibility – and then immediately wished she hadn't. She wished the race would start but there was still twenty minutes to go.

'I think I'll sign some autographs. Back in a min,' she called to Excelsior. She ran over to a crowd of waiting fans and managed to busy herself for a good ten minutes signing photos.

'Hey, you'll be beating me soon for fans,' laughed Hannibal as they walked back to prepare for the race. 'Although it seems your number one fan is waiting for you over by Excelsior.'

'What?' said Joanna. Then she saw Dominic standing next to her dragon.

'Hi, Jo!' he called. 'I wondered where you were.'

'I was signing autographs,' said Joanna quickly.

'Should have guessed, World Champion.' He smiled. 'Seems ages since I saw you. I told my nan all about seeing her photo. She was really pleased.'

He chatted so naturally about his visit that Joanna wondered how she could ever have thought he might harm their dragon egg. The more she thought about it the more ludicrous it seemed. It suddenly occurred to her that there was a very obvious explanation that she had missed – Isaac was jealous of Dominic! Here was another boy his own age who raced dragons, not just turned an egg and cleaned up after everyone.

That very thought was enough to make her flash an enormous smile at Dominic as the siren sounded announcing that all flyers and dragons should make their way to the start. Feeling happier than she had for days, Joanna almost skipped beside Excelsior.

'JoJo,' Excelsior hissed suddenly. 'I've got a confession to make, something you ought to know before we start flying.'

'Confession?' repeated Joanna uneasily. 'Like what?'

'Oh, JoJo, don't be cross. It kind of slipped out. Well, OK, it didn't *slip* out. I told her.'

'Told who what, Excelsior?' asked Joanna, looking with some alarm at her dragon.

'The thing is – you know how Hannibal's mum is here today to watch the race – and she was so kind to us last summer? I just thought that if Aurora knew how to . . .'

Joanna looked at Excelsior, beginning to understand exactly where the conversation was going.

'What have you told Aurora?'

'Only about curling, not fireballing. It was sort of my Christmas present to her. There we were, left alone in the caves while you were off having your Christmas dinner and I thought why not.' Excelsior was obviously very pleased with what he'd done. 'Aurora was *so* excited when I told her. Apparently I'm her ultimate role model. Why are you looking so worried? We can still beat them. I know we can.'

Joanna looked across at Hannibal. He flashed a huge smile and curved his hand over in a wave.

'Honestly, XL,' she sighed. 'I'm glad you told me.'

'Yeah, but think how great it's going to be when we win!' Excelsior said quickly.

'*When* – don't you mean *if*?'

'Oh, come on,' said Excelsior, 'where's your spirit of adventure? It's much more fun this way.'

'You do choose your moments, Excelsior!' replied Joanna. 'I thought you were a bit anxious to get rid of me earlier.'

'You thought I was getting at you about Cheetah, didn't you?' laughed Excelsior.

'Let's just mind-blend, shall we?' Joanna replied. 'We're going to have to pull out all the stops now!'

They had a brilliant takeoff, but next to them Hannibal and Aurora had an equally good start. The Brixton dragons were soon a good ten lengths ahead of the rest of the field and were tearing neck and neck through the air. Excelsior gave an extra flap of wing to nose ahead, only to find Aurora matching his tactics.

'Well, you wanted a race,' exclaimed Joanna, breathless from the excitement and thrill of their speed. The two dragons raced across the crisp winter sky like silver arrows cheered on by an excited crowd.

The New Year Derby was a circular two-lap race and before long the pair of Silver Spiked-Back dragons had begun the second lap. They were still neck and neck; the snaking curves of the course giving first one dragon then the other the advantage.

Within the mind-blend Joanna felt the beginnings of Excelsior's curl. She let her mind reach the top of the wave and down she soared. Out of the corner of her eye she caught sight of Hannibal and Aurora curling too. She couldn't allow them to distract her. It was going to be neck and neck for the line . . . and then suddenly with no explanation Aurora seemed to lose speed.

What was the matter? But Joanna had no time to look as she and Excelsior quickly left them behind. Ten more seconds and they were over the line. Not only had they won, but they'd smashed the existing record by over twenty-five seconds. They came into land and immediately turned to wait for Hannibal and Aurora.

'Why did they slow down like that?' Excelsior asked Joanna. 'It was just getting interesting.'

Joanna slipped off his back and, ignoring the race officials and photographers, ran over to Hannibal and Aurora.

'I tried to come down the curve of the fire wave at too steep an angle. I thought it would give me extra speed,' said Hannibal, trying to be very matter of fact, but refusing to look Joanna in the face. 'Congratulations, Jo, you won and I lost!'

'It was a good race though,' cried Joanna, rather taken aback at seeing him so crestfallen.

'That's because you won . . . again.'

Before Joanna could say anything else, Sir John Miller intervened to whisk her away to the winners' enclosure. As the gold medal was placed over her head she suddenly wondered how she would feel if she always came second. How much would the disappointment hurt? As she looked around at the other flyers she found that the day had somehow lost its shine and even Dominic Pieterson coming over to congratulate her couldn't take away the feeling that sometimes winning wasn't everything.

# 19
## TRANSFER
# PLANS

Marius King flicked the button on the remote and the television screen went blank. He was alone in the governor's office.

'So, Miss Smartypants, you won the New Year Derby in record speed. It's about time I arranged to have you taken down a peg or two. A little handicap to slow you down and give you a fright. Why, it can be a test to see if the boy does as he's told – especially after his failure to get into Marlowe's study.'

More than ever, Marius King wanted access to Marlowe's manuscripts. Was that where the brat had learned the secrets that made that Silver Spiked-Back so much faster than the other dragons? Was that why she was forbidding anyone to look at Marlowe's books?

Marius King sat back in the black leather chair. Its softness soothed him, as did the thought that the speed at which Joanna Morris flew her dragon would soon be an irrelevant detail. 'I mean even *you* can't fly if you have no dragon, little Ms Morris.'

He laughed softly to himself. Finally his plans were coming to fruition. Earlier that day he had received notification that the formula for the anti-viral cure was now ready. Of course the laboratory in question had charged twice the amount they'd originally quoted. But let them charge whatever they wanted. They would soon discover that payment had been delayed due to unforeseen circumstances and then CANCELLED. There was now only one last detail to put in place before he could unleash his revenge on the dragon-racing world.

Marius slid open the top drawer of the desk and took out a sheaf of papers. Then he rang a small bell, summoning a prison guard waiting outside the door.

'You wanted to see me, Mr King?' The prison guard's voice was nervous.

Marius King didn't answer but went on reading through his papers. This was the part he always enjoyed, playing with his victim, making them sweat a little.

He knew the guard was now desperately trying to think of all the things he could possibly have done that might have offended Mr King.

'I'm sorry about the shortage of . . .' the guard

mumbled. Marius King smiled to himself. This one was on the rack without even trying.

'Sorry, did you say something?' Marius King asked innocently. He turned back to his papers . . . and pounced. 'Smithson in cell 384 says you're undercutting him by fifty per cent on his little phone promotion. That seems a little hard. The man's only trying to make a bit of cash for when he gets out. He's asked me to have a word with you. I'm sure it's a simple misunderstanding that you can iron out between you. And Carlton over in the East wing has a similar complaint against you. In fact . . .' This was the point when he put down the papers and looked disappointed at the guard. '. . . I have here a whole list of grievances against you from my fellow inmates – enough to get you into a great deal of trouble with the powers that be. So if these "complaints" are to remain between ourselves, you are going to have to do a little favour for *me*. I can't imagine your superiors will be very pleased to hear about your *sidelines*.'

The guard looked away and gave a little cough. 'I'm sure we can come to an arrangement. What is it you want?'

'I'd like you to have me transferred to another prison,' said Marius King, making sure he stressed the word 'another'.

'I'm sure that came be organised,' said the guard,

looking almost relieved. 'Any one in particular, Mr King?'

'Oh, I'll leave the choice up to you,' smiled Marius King. 'That particular detail is irrelevant to me. No, what interests me are the dates.'

'Dates?' said the guard, looking more uncomfortable by the second. 'You mean there is more than one?'

'Of course!' said Marius King. 'That's the beauty of my plan. You see, *I* leave this prison on a certain date, everything above board, all clearly stated in the paperwork in *your* files, but the *new* prison's files won't be expecting me until . . . oh, shall we say . . . a couple of days later? All I'm really asking for is a simple clerical misunderstanding.'

The guard turned deathly pale as the truth dawned on him. 'You want me to help you escape . . .'

'Of course, you stupid man,' snapped Marius King viciously. 'You get me out of here or you'll find yourself joining me!'

The guard swallowed hard. 'Very well, Mr King. I'll see what I can do.'

'I thought you might. All right, you can go. I'll let you know the dates very shortly.'

As soon as the guard had gone, Marius King went over to the calendar on the wall.

'Countdown!' he whispered.

# 20

# FROZEN

'How come there are so many qualifying races for the Valentine Chase this year?' asked Joanna. 'We seem to have spent the whole of January racing and now it's the first week of February and we still haven't finished the qualifying rounds.'

She and Spiky Mike were in Excelsior's cave filing one of Excelsior's claws, which he'd snagged landing in the race that afternoon.

'Probably so that Sir John can boost the WDRF bank account with the entry fees from anyone and everyone,' was Spiky Mike's cynical reply. 'It's ridiculous, but there we go! At least tomorrow is the final qualifier.'

The Valentine Chase was very different to all the other races in the season. Instead of racing against each other, dragons were paired up in a draw. On a siren the first dragon would start flying, then exactly one minute later the second dragon would begin to chase after it. If the second dragon caught and placed a red marker on the first before the final siren then it was the winner, otherwise the first dragon won. It was always a very popular event with spectators – especially as the Grand Final always took place February the fourteenth – St Valentine's Day!

Just then Hannibal sauntered into Excelsior's cave waving a sheet of paper. 'I've got the draw for tomorrow. Oh, Jo, you're gonna love this. Guess who's chasing you . . .'

'Pass it here,' said Spiky Mike. He read through the draw and just grunted. 'Shouldn't be a problem.'

Hannibal gave a mock growl as Joanna snatched the paper off Spiky Mike.

Staring up at her was the name she'd known all along would be there – Dominic Pieterson.

'Think yourself lucky,' said Hannibal. 'I've got to chase Chris Perry on Tom Tom to qualify, and he's flying really well at the moment.'

Joanna looked out of her bedroom window the following morning to find a thin white carpet of snow trying to settle on the road.

'Apparently there's more on the way,' said her mother, coming into the room with a pile of ironing.

'But not until later this afternoon. It's going to be very cold.'

'Hey, Jo,' Aaron came rushing up to her. 'Present for you.' And he threw a small wet snowball at his sister.

Joanna shrieked loudly and started to chase after him. Unfortunately she had no chance to seek any snowball revenge before her mother bundled her into the van with a huge flask of hot chocolate for everyone.

'Mum, stop fussing,' said Joanna. 'We're not going to the Arctic.' But she was extremely grateful for it when they arrived at the racecourse to find the boiler in the changing rooms had broken. Her mum's hot chocolate was just what she needed to warm up again after getting changed.

She strode over to where Excelsior was enjoying the cold air by blowing steaming smoke rings, and looked around the pre-race enclosure. It was only half full of dragons.

'Where is everyone?' Joanna asked a very worried-looking race official who was glancing at his watch.

'Half the competitors are running late because of the weather,' he replied.

'Are you going to cancel the qualifiers?' asked Afra, who had overheard Joanna's question.

'No!' came the sharp reply. 'Surely you understand

the Grand Final of the Valentine Chase *has* to be on the fourteenth of February . . . Hold on, I'm just receiving the latest update.' The official listened carefully to his earpiece. 'We'll be delaying the start by half an hour.'

'If my opponent doesn't turn up, do I go through to the final sixteen automatically?' asked Joanna hopefully.

'Who are you flying against, Ms Morris?'

'Dominic Pieterson on Nemesis,' she replied as casually as possible.

'I believe they arrived about ten minutes ago,' said the official.

Just as he finished speaking Joanna caught sight of Trix Dawson leading Nemesis into the enclosure. A few moments later Dominic came running out of the changing rooms, flapping his arms up and down in an attempt to get warm.

'Hi, Jo. I can't believe they're making us race in the snow. I thought we'd never get here – the roads were terrible. We skidded twice! And all that so you can beat me.'

Before Joanna could think of a suitable reply Dominic's trainer commented sharply, 'Dominic that's not the attitude I want to hear before your race.'

Dominic mouthed the words silently, mimicking his trainer and making Joanna laugh, before adding,

'Come on, let's go and watch from the stand where our trainers can't get us. I wish I was going to be here for the Grand Final; I really wanted to see all the hearts and stuff they use to decorate the stands with.'

They slipped into the spectator stand as Hannibal opened the afternoon racing. Despite his worries about Chris Perry's form, Aurora was much faster than the other dragon, Tom Tom. Joanna felt her heart give a little skip as she watched them spiral into a dive. They were curling in the spiral and the speed was amazing.

Quick as a flash, Hannibal placed the tag on Tom Tom's backside and the race was over. As he came in to land he looked over to where Joanna was sitting and curled his hand in a wave. Hannibal had obviously sorted out his problem of timing the curl – and wanted Joanna to know.

Dominic and Joanna watched a couple more races before his trainer discovered their whereabouts and insisted that Dominic return to the flyers' enclosure.

'I thought I told you not to go wandering about till after your race. And Joanna, you look freezing. Dominic, everyone will say you're trying to sabotage the competition – run and get Joanna your scarf.'

To Joanna's amazement Dominic looked at Trix and snapped, 'No! I don't want to.'

'It's OK, I'm fine,' replied Joanna, trying hard not to show that she felt embarrassed and a little bit hurt that Dominic should have refused this simple request. Dominic turned to Joanna looking quite distressed. Then without further explanation he shrugged his shoulders and mumbled, 'Yeah, of course, Trix. I'll go and get it.'

He ran off quickly and Joanna found herself left with Trix Dawson.

'Really, I'm fine,' replied Joanna, hoping that Dominic wouldn't be too long. 'In fact, I need to get ready for my race, so if you'll excuse me.'

Joanna started to walk away, but Dominic came running up.

'Here, Jo, my scarf.'

Joanna held out her hand for it. It was spotted like a cheetah, with metallic gold threads running through it. Even now he seemed reluctant to hand it over.

'Well, give it to her, Dominic,' said his trainer. 'It's not going to help her in your hand.'

'*There* you are!' An angry voice behind Joanna made her groan. Spiky Mike was storming straight towards her. 'I've been looking for you everywhere. It's only ten minutes until your race and you should be preparing to fly, not playing with your boyfriend!'

Joanna spun round to face her trainer and glared at him hard. Trust Spiky Mike to embarrass her like that. She turned round again and took the scarf from Dominic, saying loudly, 'Thanks, Dominic.

It's nice that some people are bothered that I'm freezing cold.'

She ran past Spiky Mike, ignoring him completely, and wrapped the scarf around her neck.

'Sorry, XL,' said Joanna, as she climbed onto Excelsior's back. 'But I've had just about enough of snotty trainers. Spiky Mike just called Dominic my boyfriend right in front of him! I've never been so embarrassed in my life.'

As they settled down to prepare for the race, Joanna caught sight of Hannibal taking a seat in the spectator stand. Obviously he was doing his homework to see if she and Excelsior had any new tricks up their sleeve.

'Hey, XL, Hannibal's checking up on us.' But to Joanna's surprise Excelsior wasn't listening, he was twisting and turning his neck from side to side.

'What's the matter, XL?' asked Joanna immediately.

'I've suddenly got a terrible itch all along the side of my neck.' 'Do you think it's the cold?' asked Joanna, trying to scratch the silver scales by rubbing very hard with her glove. 'Let's get this race over with and then we can warm up properly.'

As soon as Joanna went into the mind-blend with Excelsior she felt the irritation on Excelsior's neck. It was really painful – like sharp jabbing needles. As a result they got off to a pretty poor start. By the time the second siren sounded to announce that they were being chased, the pain in Excelsior's neck had grown so intense that it was only with difficulty that she could keep the mind-blend. They were flying slower and slower. Joanna was desperately trying to keep an eye on Nemesis. He was getting dangerously close behind them. They were going to have to dive quickly to avoid being caught.

'Dive! You must dive now, XL!' cried Joanna. But XL didn't move. He just kept on flying in a straight line. The next moment she felt a thump and she knew they'd been tagged.

They'd lost!

From down below she could hear the shocked cries of the spectators. Some of them were booing! Joanna pushed away all her disappointment. She needed to find out what was the matter with Excelsior. She landed on the far side of the field away from the crowd of officials and spectators. Flakes of snow were starting to drift slowly down from a white sky. But Joanna ignored them and started examining Excelsior's neck.

'Now, XL, where exactly does it hurt?' asked Joanna. 'I can't see any marks or cuts or blisters, or anything like that.'

'Just below where you rest your head in the mind-blend,' said Excelsior apprehensively as Joanna took off her gloves to feel the silver scales. There seemed to be raised ridges like thin weals running across his neck. They were almost invisible.

'Do they hurt when I touch them?'

'The pain's not so bad now we've stopped flying. More like a dull throb,' said Excelsior. 'Let's get back and show Spiky Mike.'

They walked back over the field, which was fast disappearing under a blanket of fresh snow, to where Spiky Mike was waiting at the gate.

'Just keep me waiting in the freezing cold, won't you? What the heck do you think you were doing over on the other side of the field? So you lost. Hard luck! Now go and get changed and hurry up about it.'

Joanna stared in horror at her trainer.

'How *dare* you!' she screamed. 'It's Excelsior! Something's the matter with his neck! Look!' She threw off her gloves and started to show him the raised marks.

'Not here, Joanna,' snapped Spiky Mike. 'I can't see anything in this snow, or this light.'

Joanna hurried Excelsior to where the van was waiting for them. 'OK, now show me.' said Spiky Mike shining a torch onto Excelsior's neck.

'Here!' said Joanna feeling along the silver scales – except she couldn't feel the raised bits at all. Excelsior's neck felt quite smooth and normal.

'But there were weals, like thin ridges!' Joanna

started feeling frantically along the whole side of Excelsior's neck. 'Look, feel . . .'

But Spiky Mike just stood there staring, not at Excelsior's neck, but at Joanna.

'Losing is bad enough but making up excuses for it is contemptible.' He walked off in disgust.

Joanna stood there stunned, unable to move.

'But we didn't imagine it, did we, XL? I mean they were there. How does your neck feel now?'

'Quite normal,' said Excelsior quietly. 'I don't understand it any more than you do. All I know was that as soon as we started racing something was really hurting my neck.'

Joanna walked slowly down the ramp and made her way over to the changing rooms. She was rather relieved that no one was hanging around. At least she didn't have to listen to anyone's comments or, worse, their false sympathy. They were all probably gossiping about her behind her back – how the World Champion had lost to a novice. She looked down at Dominic's scarf. It was lying where she'd dropped it on top of her jacket. She picked it up.

'Oh, why did it have to be you, Dominic?'

'Joanna?' she heard Afra's voice calling from the doorway. 'Are you OK?'

Joanna found she couldn't turn round to face Afra, as the reality of the afternoon swept over her.

'I'll be out in a minute,' she called, adding suddenly, 'Afra, could you do me a big favour . . .' She held out the scarf. 'Could you give this to Dominic? He lent it to me because I was cold . . . I don't want . . .'

Afra nodded in understanding. 'Of course, Jo. I'll go and give it to his trainer.'

Joanna finished changing, and packed up her flying gear. She knew she was taking so long that Spiky Mike would be in an even worse mood by the time she appeared. Oh well, let him wait. She started to fold up her jacket into her bag, when suddenly she noticed its dragon-skin collar was covered in a series of thin, tiny raised lines – just like the ones she'd seen on Excelsior's neck.

What on earth had made them? Still, at least she had proof to show Spiky Mike. She stuffed the jacket into her bag and ran out to the waiting van.

# 21
# REVELATIONS

The caves were strangely quiet when Joanna arrived the next morning – until she realised that everyone was keeping out of the way, finding jobs at the other end of the caves to Spiky Mike's office.

'Well I've done nothing wrong,' said Joanna to herself as she prepared to confront him. She knocked, waited a moment and then pushed open the door defiantly. It took her a moment to register what she was looking at. Spiky Mike's desk was like some monstrous rubbish dump. There were old coffee mugs, dangerously high piles of papers, files and magazines, and his laptop and printer were buried somewhere deep in the debris. Under his desk the waste bin was overflowing. That was nothing new. Far worse was Spiky Mike himself – he looked terrible. She saw him push a blanket behind his chair. Had he slept there?

Any concern Joanna might have felt was gone as soon as he opened his mouth.

'Were you trying to lose? Excelsior was barely moving. And if you must start fancying a fellow flyer at least find someone with a tiny bit of talent. The boy's pathetic.'

Joanna stomped into the room, banging the door shut behind her. She was angry, embarrassed and most of all fed up with her trainer for not even trying to hear what she had to say.

'How dare you! I did *not* lose on purpose. I told you, Excelsior was in pain and I *did* find these raised ridges on his neck . . . and on my jacket too. Anyway, so what if I like Dominic Pieterson – there's no crime in that!'

'There is if it stops you flying properly.'

'Is that what you think? That I lost on purpose because I like Dominic? You know, sometimes I wonder if you know me at all. Afra does. She listens to me. She asked me if I was all right yesterday. Did you? NO! And have you asked to see my jacket?'

'What on earth has your jacket got to do with anything?' scoffed Spiky Mike.

'You see, you don't listen – I just told you I found the same raised weals on my jacket that were on Excelsior.'

'So show me your jacket – let's see these amazing raised marks that made you lose a race.'

Joanna pulled out her jacket and pointed at the thin raised lines.

'And this is supposed to prove what?' said Spiky Mike disparagingly.

'That something hurt Excelsior!' insisted Joanna.

Spiky Mike didn't say anything.

'What! You think I'm lying?' Joanna could hear her voice getting louder. 'What is it with you this morning? I'm sorry I lost! Yes, I'm embarrassed about losing, but most of all I'm fed up with YOU!' Joanna was screaming now, she just couldn't help it. 'Oh you're all nice when I win, or when Excelsior learns something new, but the rest of the time you're horrible to me. Well know this – I hate you being my trainer. I wish Afra was. I've been wishing it all season.'

Joanna stared angrily at Spiky Mike, watching his face change from red to white. Why had she said that? Was it true? Yes. Yes it was and she hoped it hurt. It must have done, because Spiky Mike suddenly stood up, sweeping everything off his desk and onto the floor. Cups smashed, splashing their dregs, and a great snowstorm of papers flew to every corner of the room.

'Fine!' he shouted back. 'That's fine. Why should I carry on training a teenager who is completely oblivious to the fact that I'm slogging my guts out just so she can moon over some pathetic boy? It obviously means nothing to you. Let Afra be your trainer if you think she understands you so much better than me.' He grabbed his jacket and without a backward glance walked out of the office.

Joanna sat there stunned, looking at the strewn-up papers and the blanket and dirty cups. What was that all about? She knew losing the race was bad, and OK she'd said some terrible things. But she'd never seen Spiky Mike lose it *completely*.

'Joanna, what . . . where's Mike?' Afra suddenly appeared in the doorway looking aghast at the devastation in front of her. 'What on earth happened?'

'I'm not sure. Spiky Mike was so angry . . . I was so horrid . . . I said I hated him.' Joanna suddenly started to sob uncontrollably.

Afra waited patiently until Joanna had calmed down enough to tell her the gist of the argument.

'He's got a lot on his plate, Jo,' she said. 'What with training you, supervising Isaac, having to keep on top of the paperwork and all the time worrying about Agnes.'

'But I don't understand why he wouldn't believe me about Excelsior's neck,' said Joanna. 'Why would I make something like that up? And I have not "mooned" over Dominic!'

Afra smiled. 'No, you haven't. I don't understand any more than you why he's *so* upset.'

'Perhaps I can throw some light on the matter,' came a voice from the doorway.

Joanna and Afra turned to see Mr Hogan. He wheeled his chair into the office. 'I'm sorry. I didn't mean to eavesdrop. I'd just come to see why Joanna was late for class and I couldn't help but overhear.' He sighed. 'I think the time has come for me to tell you why I'm in a wheelchair.'

Joanna and Afra looked at each other, wondering what on earth Mr Hogan was going to say.

'About ten years ago I was in an accident. Did Mike ever tell you about it, Afra?'

Afra looked at him blankly.

'I was eighteen and had managed to get myself a job in the West Sussex Dragon Caves for the summer holidays. You know, the usual thing, feeding the dragons, cleaning out troughs.' He smiled sadly at the memory. 'I had the most fantastic summer of my life. There was a whole crowd of us including Spiky Mike – although he was just Mike in those days – and his sister, Lucy . . .'

'Spiky Mike's got a sister!' exclaimed Joanna, completely surprised.

'I didn't know you knew Lucy,' said Afra quietly, looking closely at Mr Hogan.

Mr Hogan's eyes went all misty. 'She was gorgeous. I think all the boys were in love with her – me included. Spiky Mike was a typical brother though, said he couldn't see what all the fuss was about . . . You haven't heard all this before?' Mr Hogan looked questioningly at Afra.

'He could never bring himself to tell me,' said Afra. 'But I've always been curious.'

'Tell you *what*?' said Joanna, both exasperated and intrigued about where this conversation was heading.

'I'm only telling you now because I think it will explain things . . .' continued Mr Hogan.

'Of course,' said Afra.

*So go on*, thought Joanna. *Tell us. I want to know everything.* She strongly suspected that Afra did too.

Mr Hogan was anxious to continue.

'Most of us were just helping out at the caves but Spiky Mike was an apprentice trainer to his sister who was a novice flyer. Her dragon was an English Green called Boudicca, a rather temperamental dragon who was showing real potential. Well, at the end of the holiday the owner threw a party for everyone. Just before the party finished someone suggested that we finish off the celebrations with a night fly on the dragons. We all rushed down to the caves. There were only seven dragons and ten of us. Rather than leave anyone behind we decided to share dragons. I couldn't believe my luck when Lucy asked me if I'd like to fly with her on Boudicca. Of course I said yes – what I didn't know was that Spiky Mike, as Lucy's trainer, had forbidden her to take anyone with her. But Lucy had other ideas. She was always complaining about how bossy her brother was and how he was always telling her what to do.'

'What a surprise!' said Joanna sarcastically.

Afra frowned and shook her head at Joanna. 'What happened, Ambrose?'

'We were last to leave so that her brother wouldn't know what she was up to. I can still remember the moment when Boudicca took off. I was sitting behind Lucy. I'd never travelled so fast in my whole life. The ground just fell away beneath us and we were surrounded by a dome of stars in a clear black night. Lucy was a great flyer and Boudicca quickly caught up with the other dragons, and then overtook them. Soon we were alone in the night sky. I thought I was in heaven!

'Then, just like that, the weather turned on us and there we were flying into a great storm. I've never seen rain like it. The lightning flashed nonstop all around us. It was terrifying – I thought we'd be hit so I started to panic and broke out of the mind-blend. I was hanging onto Lucy for dear life. Somehow she managed to keep the mind-blend going. But we were losing height rapidly. We were heading for this great copse of trees and we hit the treetops at speed. Boudicca's wing ripped and we fell . . .' Mr Hogan closed his eyes, shuddering at the memory.

'But you survived,' said Joanna slowly.

'*I* survived . . .' Mr Hogan's voice broke as he said this. He sat there staring at them. '. . . it was Lucy who died. Spiky Mike found us. He'd seen us pass him and had come chasing after us. He saved my life. He never blamed me once for what happened to his sister. Said it was his fault for flying off without her. He's never flown on a dragon since . . .' Mr Hogan fell into silence as if reliving his terrible memories.

Joanna knew that Afra was crying but she could only sit there staring at the mess on the floor, hearing again and again the words: 'It was Lucy who died.'

'Seeing you lose that race, thinking you were messing about with Dominic and putting everything at risk must have brought it all back,' said Mr Hogan.

'But I was not messing about with Dominic,' insisted Joanna. 'Spiky Mike was wrong and he didn't even try to listen to me. He *never* listens to me!'

'He might not always get it right, but he uses a great deal of time and energy trying to help you,' said Mr Hogan gently. 'Did you know that he arranged for me to fly back from Japan because he particularly wanted you to have a teacher who would help you with the subjects Vincent would have taught?'

'Like Latin?' said Joanna.

'Like Latin and later on chemistry and philosophy and . . .'

'. . . all the things I'd need to know to understand Vincent's manuscripts.' Joanna looked guiltily at Mr Hogan.

'He did that even though every time he sees me he must be reminded of his sister.'

'Why did you say yes?' asked Joanna.

Mr Hogan looked a little embarrassed. 'I'm not as high-minded as Spiky Mike. I have to confess I had a more selfish reason. Forgive me, Joanna, but when Spiky Mike told me about the nature of Vincent's manuscripts, I was rather hoping I might discover something to help me walk again.'

Joanna stared at her tutor. 'Walk again?'

Mr Hogan laughed bitterly. 'Sometimes I feel it's wanting too much! I still feel guilty about surviving the accident. Of course I've never mentioned it to Spiky Mike . . . I'm far too much of a coward.'

Joanna felt as if she was just seeing him properly for the first time. *Which I am!* she thought. All his learning couldn't stop him from longing to walk once more. She suddenly had a vision of Vincent scouring his bookshelves to find some way to help Mr Hogan.

'You can look at them,' she said suddenly. 'At Vincent's books. I know he would want you to . . . I don't know if you'll find anything, but you can try.'

A look of gratitude swept over Mr Hogan's face and he appeared so hopeful that Joanna felt ashamed at her previous reluctance.

'Thank you, Joanna. It is very generous of you. Now come back to class and leave Afra to contact Spiky Mike.'

After the high drama of the morning the rest of the day was comfortingly dull.

Even geography, Joanna's least favourite subject, seemed a pleasant and easy distraction. Afterwards she hurried to see Excelsior, only to find Isaac waiting for her.

'I think I know what made the marks on Excelsior's neck – he told me about them this morning, when I was feeding him,' he said quickly, checking to see if Joanna looked annoyed. 'I think Excelsior had an allergic reaction to something. I went and looked it up. Don't worry – not in one of Vincent's books.' He opened an old battered book and pointed to one of the entries. 'Look at this.'

*Urticara draconis (rare), severe localised reactions include: raised weals, acute skin irritation and an intense burning sensation. Extremely painful.*

*WARNING: a dragon's sense of direction may be seriously effected. Do not fly.*

Isaac pointed to the following section. 'It gives a remedy too: *Bathe affected area in freezing cold water to soothe and neutralise.* It must have been the snow falling that neutralised it so quickly. No wonder they'd disappeared by the time you showed them to Spiky Mike.'

Joanna read the entry again. 'But this *urticara draconis* – where could it come from? It says it's rare. And what about my jacket?'

'Did you touch or wear anything out of the ordinary. Did a fan give you a gift or something?'

Joanna felt a wave of horror creep over her. Surely it couldn't be . . . ? Not that. Not Dominic's scarf! She felt sick just thinking about it. That was why Trix had been so keen for Dominic to get the scarf – and why Dominic had been so reluctant to give it to her. It was a plan to help Dominic beat her. But that was cheating!

Cheat . . . Joanna stopped. Was his name Cheetah or Cheat-er?

'I can't think of anything in particular,' she lied to Isaac – *he must never find out the truth.* 'Thanks anyway – at least this proves to Spiky Mike that I wasn't making it up.'

Isaac nodded and left Joanna alone with Excelsior.

'Did you know that Dominic was a cheat, XL? Why didn't you tell me?'

'I only suspected,' came the reply. 'And I didn't want to upset you.'

Joanna hugged her dragon tightly. 'Everything's falling apart, XL – I've lost my race, my trainer and now my new friend . . . Oh, what am I going to do?'

# 22
## A CLEAR
# VIEW

Spiky Mike rang Joanna's parents that same evening to inform them that he was taking a couple of weeks' holiday and that he'd let them know his future work plans when he got back.

'Spiky Mike's not going to leave, is he?' Joanna had asked in dismay. She hadn't really thought his walking out was serious. 'I mean, he will come back?'

'We're dealing with one thing at a time,' said her father in a grave voice. 'For now, Giovanni has offered to have you and Excelsior to stay so that Afra and Hannibal can concentrate on the Valentine Chase and not waste time worrying about you.'

'But if I'm in Wales, what about my lessons? And what about my training?' asked Joanna.

'Mr Hogan has agreed to make it your half-term break and Giovanni will make sure that you and

Excelsior get some sort of training. It's not perfect, but it's the best we can come up with at short notice. He'll pick up you and Excelsior tomorrow morning, so you'd better go and pack.'

Any other time Joanna would have been delighted to visit Giovanni and Lucia's dragon sanctuary, but not now. She wanted to stay in Brixton with . . . who? There wasn't anybody she felt really cared about her.

Joanna arrived at the caves the following morning to wait for Giovanni feeling very sorry for herself. She walked slowly past Agnes's office. It was all dark and shut up. She hadn't seen Agnes for over a month because she had gone to recuperate with a daughter who lived outside London, although she had written her a nice letter congratulating her on winning the New Year Derby. Joanna knew she should give her a call to see how she was, but things between them had been so strained since Isaac had started egg turning that she kept putting it off.

The light was on in Vincent's study though. Mr Hogan had obviously started going through Vincent's papers and books. She stopped outside the door. There were excited voices talking about some strange Latin words she'd never heard of. Isaac must be helping him. She couldn't bear to see *that*! Quickly she walked down to Aurora's cave. As she entered she found Hannibal and Afra talking animatedly about tactics for the forthcoming race. Those two never seemed to argue.

Joanna felt a pang of loneliness. Everybody was busy . . . and happy. It was as though she didn't belong at the Brixton Caves any more.

'I just came to wish you luck in the Valentine Chase and to say goodbye,' was all she could say.

Hannibal stood there and sighed. 'Hey, Jo, you know the race won't be the same without you and XL. And don't worry, I'll take out the Cheetah for you. The Brixton Caves will bring home the cup and then later in the summer we'll have our own final. Oh, come on, don't cry . . .'

But poor Joanna was in tears.

'Tell . . . Spik . . . y . . . Mike . . . I'm . . . so . . . rr . . . y . . .' she blubbered to Afra.

'I will,' said Afra brightly. 'And you have a great time with Giovanni and Lucia.'

Joanna tried to smile, but somehow she knew that Afra's enthusiasm was as false as her own smile.

The mountain was lost in thick cloud, and heavy wet rain was sweeping across the Welsh countryside making everything look bleak and forlorn as Giovanni pulled up in front of the large pebble-dashed house to drop off Joanna before continuing up the mountain to the dragon caves to settle Excelsior.

Lucia ran out with an umbrella and hurried Joanna into the kitchen.

'Look how you've grown,' she cried. 'But, oh, how pale and so skinny!'

Joanna knew exactly what was coming next. Last time she visited the dragon sanctuary she'd spent half the time stuffing her face on Lucia's amazing cooking. True to form Lucia put a huge bowl of soup and some freshly baked bread in front of her.

'No questions, no news, nothing, until after you have eaten!'

But even after lunch neither Giovanni nor Lucia asked Joanna anything about the events in the Brixton Caves or mentioned Spiky Mike's name, which Joanna found strange. These were two of Spiky Mike's closest and most loyal friends. Instead they seemed abnormally talkative about what Joanna would be doing during her stay, especially about making the most of training in a mountainous environment. What were they hiding?

Joanna wasn't sure if she was brave enough to ask.

The weather cleared sufficiently in the afternoon for Joanna to take Excelsior out for a fly round the mountain. It was just what she needed. Her dragon was as keen as she was to fly as fast and as high as possible.

'Come on, XL, no one can get us up here,' cried Joanna.

They didn't think, they didn't feel, they just flew faster and faster. They fireballed, they curled, they tore across the sky and plunged earthwards in twisting spirals. It felt so good – so normal! It was only as the light drained from the sky that they came in to land.

Giovanni was waiting down in the landing field. He'd obviously been watching them for some time.

'What?' said Joanna, somewhat taken back by the look on Giovanni's face.

'I've never really watched you fly on Excelsior. I mean I've watched your races on TV and I remember your first flight here, but I've never seen you *really* fly together. Not like that! It's amazing. He really has done a brilliant job. It would be a shame if it all changed.' Joanna looked at Giovanni. By 'he' she knew Giovanni meant Spiky Mike. Did Giovanni know something she didn't?

Any further conversation became impossible as a heavy squall of rain forced them to hurry back to the caves to start the evening routine and Joanna was soon busy with feeding Excelsior. When she'd finished, she asked her dragon what he made of what Giovanni had said, and was shocked by his reply.

'Perhaps Spiky Mike wants out. I mean look at it from his point of view – what can he teach me?'

'XL, that's a bit pompous of you!'

'Not if it's true. I'm not denying he's a brilliant trainer. He is, but now he's wasting his time. He's done his job too well and he knows it.'

Joanna thought about what Excelsior had said. Could it be true? Every time she flew up the mountain, she remembered some lesson Spiky Mike had taught her. She remembered how difficult she'd found the exercises at first, but now she could do it all standing on her head. The only new thing she'd learned this season was fireballing and it was Excelsior who'd discovered that.

'But Spiky Mike keeps me focused,' Joanna insisted to Excelsior. 'So even if you don't need him – I do!'

'I wasn't thinking of *us*,' Excelsior remarked quietly. 'I was thinking of Spiky Mike and what *he* needs.'

They were sitting together on the summit of the mountain. Joanna was sheltering between Excelsior's front legs, with her back resting on his belly so that she could be warmed by her dragon's fire. It was a clear winter's day, the air was crisp and the light was so sharp that they could see for miles to the blue sea; a perfect reflection of azure sky. It was completely silent except for the occasional bleating of sheep.

Joanna looked sadly up at Excelsior. 'Do you know

what I hate about dragon racing? It's what competition does to everyone. I really liked Dominic, and all the time he was just making friends with me so he could beat me. And look how upset Hannibal was when he lost against us, or how jealous Afra was when Spiky Mike didn't tell her about fireballing. I mean, is it like that for dragons?'

'Of course,' admitted Excelsior. 'I think we're worse than humans. Racing dragons live to race – to win! Look at Prometheus. He was even prepared to destroy his flyer.'

'But Prometheus wasn't like any other dragon I've ever met,' shuddered Joanna, remembering Hannibal's unconscious body at the feet of that green monster. 'I do hope Hannibal wins the Valentine Chase.'

'And there was I hoping it would be Aurora,' replied Excelsior mischievously. 'If she wins she might actually shut up for change. I tell you, it's like having a pesky kid sister.'

Joanna looked at him in surprise. 'But Aurora's the quietest dragon I've ever met! She hardly speaks to me.'

'Only because she's in awe of you. You're her heroine,' said Excelsior proudly. 'Meanwhile, she's been pestering me this past two weeks from morning till night to tell her about fireballing! Not that I let *that* little secret out of the bag. But you just watch her. She'll leave the rest of them standing . . . and I'll be like a proud big brother!'

# 23

## PHASE TWO

The black car cut its engine and slid silently down to the bottom of the hill. Inside, the driver kept glancing nervously around. The place was deserted and the moonless sky hid the car in shadow. No one could possibly know he was there. And anyway the CCTV cameras had been switched off a good thirty minutes previously.

'Come on, come on,' muttered the driver, glancing nervously down at his watch. A few moments later the mobile phone on the dashboard started to vibrate – there was the signal.

The driver released the central locking on the car, the locks flipped up and a heavy figure slipped quickly into the back seat. Immediately the driver started the engine and slowly the car moved away. They drove in silence for a good ten minutes, then the passenger pulled off his balaclava and laughed out loud.

'Good to see you, Mr King,' said the driver, looking in the rear-view mirror. 'It's been a long time.'

'Too long,' agreed Marius King, pouring a tumbler of malt whisky from the drinks cabinet. 'How long before we reach our destination?'

'A couple of hours, sir,' came the driver's reply. 'I trust you have everything you need? The briefcase you asked for is on the floor.'

Marius King opened the case and took out a phone.

'No one can trace this, can they?' he asked the driver sharply.

'Of course not, Mr King. All your instructions have been followed to the letter.'

Marius King touched a button and a glass partition slid up silently. His time in prison had made him suspicious of even his most loyal employees. Now was the most dangerous time of all. But after today no one, but no one, would be able to stop him.

He keyed a number into the phone. Whoever was at the other end was obviously waiting for the call because they answered immediately.

'Phase Two is going according to plan,' said Marius. 'I'll be at our rendezvous point in a couple of hours.'

He rang off and took a newspaper out of the briefcase. He flicked quickly through until he found, halfway down one of the middle pages, the list of dragons and flyers competing in the finals of the Valentine Chase. Much to his annoyance he'd had to forgo watching the final heats due to a snap inspection of the prison by a government minister.

'*Tim Button on Tiger Lily* – so after all these years you've qualified for a final. What a shame it will be your last. And there you are again *Lucy Bell on Sasparilla*! How will you feel about my little shake-up? My advice is, next time choose a dragon with a sensible name . . .' Marius King stopped for a second before proceeding. '*Hannibal Henry Oliver*!' He half hissed half spat out the name. 'Traitor! After all I did for you. And flying such an inferior breed! Hannibal, I created a Jewel dragon for you. How could you sink so low? Now where are the brat and that skinny silver snake of hers?' He quickly ran his eyes over the names of the dragons and flyers again, before screwing the page it into a tight ball. 'No!' he insisted. 'That cannot be right.'

He picked up the phone and redialled the previous number.

'Joanna Morris – I can't see her name on the list for the Valentine Chase . . . *She what?* I said slow her down, not take her out, you fool! So where is she now? In Wales . . . Of course we're still going ahead with my plans for the Valentine Chase. That event is just the beginning!'

Marius King closed his eyes. A few hiccups along the way could only be expected. Now that he was free from that vile prison he would soon be in absolute control. He sank further back into the soft leather of the car seat and laughed. As far as the prison authorities were concerned he was still in their care. His plan had worked perfectly. By the time anyone had noticed he was no longer a prisoner, he would be far, far away.

As the car sped along the motorway, the first light of a February dawn started to brighten the sky. A sharp touch of frost glittered in the fields and outlined the bare black hedges in silver. Such beauty was lost on the man. Marius King was staring up at the clear skies. It was going to be a perfect day for racing – a perfect day to exact his revenge!

Before long the car turned off the motorway and, following a series of small country roads, turned into a small field where a large dragon transport van was parked next to a caravan. Marius got out and quickly disappeared inside the caravan not waiting to see his previous transport vanish into the winding lanes of the countryside. Twenty minutes later he reappeared, transformed by a wig, beard and suit complete with a red rose button hole, followed by a woman.

'Ready for the races, Mr . . . ?' said Marius King's accomplice.

'George Smith will do, dear sister. Although as your new *boyfriend* you might want to call me *Georgie*,' sneered Marius. 'I'm escorting you to the races. It's our first date! The red rose is a nice romantic touch, don't you think?'

'It's not a game, Marius,' Trix Dawson snapped back angrily. 'It's been fine for you sitting there giving out orders. *I'm* the one who's been running all the risks. Have you any idea how much work has been involved?'

'Risks!' roared Marius King. 'Was there no risk for me blackmailing prison governors and guards? And why are you complaining? You're doing very well out of this financially!'

A boy's pale, tired face suddenly appeared at the back of the dragon transport van. He stared over at Marius King before calling out to his trainer, 'What's happening? Who's he?'

'Shut up, Dominic, get back in the van!'

Trix went over and slammed the door shut.

'My nan . . . what have you done to my nan?' Dominic shouted from inside.

'I told you, Dominic, if you want what's best for your nan you'll do exactly as you're told. Now shut up and sit down.'

Marius King followed his sister into the front of the van.

'Ready to begin Phase Three? Oh I am *so* looking forward to this.'

# 24
## WE ALL
## FALL DOWN

'Hurry up, Joanna,' called Giovanni. 'At this rate you'll be cleaning up Excelsior's lunch things at suppertime. The race coverage starts in ten minutes.'

Joanna knew she was being particularly slow, but only because she was trying to avoid having to watch Dominic in the pre-race interviews.

'Did you know I met Lucia at the Valentine Chase?' said Giovanni as they walked back to the house.

'Did you?' said Joanna, genuinely curious. 'What happened?'

'Lucia was on a work experience placement as part of her catering diploma and was working in one of the refreshment marquees. I was supposed to be on duty in the emergency medical tent. Instead I spent the day getting endless cups of coffee for everyone else. Didn't see a single dragon the whole day!'

Lucia had arranged the sofas and provided a whole selection of snacks and drinks, but Joanna just stood watching by the door so she could escape if Dominic came into view. Giovanni sank down on the sofa next to Lucia and took an enormous handful of popcorn just in time to see the tail end of an interview with Sir John Miller.

'You certainly didn't miss anything there,' Lucia yawned. 'Can a man be more boring . . . ooh look at the decorations! What beautiful roses. They must have cost a fortune . . . and isn't that Mouse, over there on the second row? The one with the $H_2O$ Is Cool T-shirt?'

'Where?' said Joanna, unable to resist seeing her friend. 'Yes it is! Look she's put pink streaks in her hair. She said she was going to support both her sister and Hannibal!' Joanna didn't add that Mouse had also said she would boo Dominic in front of the camera if she got the opportunity. Joanna had told Mouse *everything.*

Then suddenly there was Dominic, standing in front of the camera with his trainer. Joanna stared. He looked . . . terrible. His hair was a mess, like he hadn't combed it. And his jacket, his lovely jacket, was missing beads and sequins. It was painfully embarrassing to watch as he mumbled unintelligible answers. She couldn't bear to look until the camera cut to where the first race was about to start between Mouse's sister, Emilia Chatfield on her dragon Tambourine Man and Tim Button on Tiger Lily. Joanna quickly went and sat in the armchair nearest the television – this was far too exciting to miss.

'Ooh, look at her time!' shouted Joanna excitedly as Emilia quickly tagged Tiger Lily. 'She'll be up for fastest catch with that. That'll be a challenge for Hannibal. He's next, isn't he?'

The start of Hannibal's race had to be delayed briefly. His fan club were out in force and were screaming so loudly that Sir John Miller had to make an announcement over the loudspeaker, saying that if the girls did not stop then Hannibal would be disqualified. Silence descended immediately and the race began. The Brixton team were being chased by a guest Russian team. They were fast but Aurora was in her element. Hannibal's control in the spiral made Joanna want to burst with pride, until she overheard Giovanni whisper to Lucia, 'He told me he was going to coach Hannibal with that move.'

'Don't you mean she?' Joanna turned to ask Giovanni.

Lucia threw a quick glance at her husband and shook her head. Joanna saw it.

Giovanni quickly replied, 'Of course *she* – just a slip of the tongue.'

But Joanna knew he was lying. It was obvious now – the *he* in question was Spiky Mike!

'Spiky Mike's been helping coach Hannibal?' asked Joanna feeling not only shocked but hurt.

As Hannibal came in to land on Aurora, Joanna suddenly caught sight of Spiky Mike standing next to Afra. The pair of them looked so happy.

Giovanni saw the look of dismay on Joanna's face. 'Afra asked him, because it's one of his specialities.'

'So when everyone said he's on holiday, what they really meant was on holiday *from me*,' Joanna said quietly.

'Come on, Joanna,' said Giovanni. 'You know he's there to support Afra.'

'And that means helping Hannibal as well, does it?' said Joanna crossly.

'He's supporting the Brixton Caves,' replied Lucia. 'And that means you!'

Giovanni was about to say something too, when something on the television made him call out, 'What on earth . . . ?'

They all immediately turned back to the television screen where a dragon was lurching awkwardly through the sky. Its wings were hardly moving and its tail hung down, perilously near the heads of the watching crowd, who were now screaming in terror.

'Which dragon is that?' gasped Lucia.

'Nemesis!' said Joanna, instantly recognising the huge golden dragon. 'That's Nemesis!' She could see Dominic clinging tightly to the dragon's neck. He was swaying from side to side as if he were about to be flung off. 'He's broken the mind-blend,' she cried out. 'He'll fall . . .'

Nemesis was now flying so low he barely cleared the stand. He swooped up into the air at the last moment just missing one of the banks of Valentine's Day flowers. Somehow Dominic managed to cling on but below him screaming crowds were running in every direction, climbing over seats, pushing over each other in their bid to escape the dragon. Suddenly a flash of silver was streaking through the air straight towards Nemesis, who was now wildly spiralling through the air, lurching this way and that.

'Aurora!' gasped Joanna. 'But that's not Hannibal . . .'

'What the?' cried Giovanni. 'It's . . .'

'Spiky Mike!' said Joanna in astonishment. They stood in helpless silence watching Spiky Mike flying alongside Nemesis. He grabbed hold of the petrified Dominic and dragged him onto Aurora. Just in time they pulled out of reach of Nemesis's tail thrashing the air wildly. The exhausted dragon was gasping for breath. Thick black smoke poured from his nostrils until suddenly Nemesis wretched, spewing out thick grey phlegm into the air. It splattered over Aurora, covering her in sticky steaming globs.

Dominic let out a cry. He was sliding off. Spiky Mike caught his arm and held him firm until they landed. Safe on the ground they stared upwards to where Nemesis was writhing in agony. Finally with a strangled, rasping cry the once-magnificent golden dragon plunged to the ground. Nemesis jerked and shuddered, then fell still. He was dead.

The emergency services leapt into action and cordoned off the dragon. Sir John Miller pushed his way towards the nearest television camera and stood in front, blocking its view as it tried to get a close-up of the dead dragon. Suddenly the camera cut away to Spiky Mike and Dominic. They were both covered in thick sticky muck.

Trix Dawson immediately appeared at Dominic's side. She put her arm around him and seemed to be pulling him away when suddenly Dominic grabbed hold of Spiky Mike. He still looked terrified but before he could say a word his trainer turned to the camera and said, 'We really can't thank Spiky Mike enough, but after such a traumatic experience Dominic is particularly anxious to see his grandmother – aren't you, Dominic?'

Dominic's arms fell limply to his side and he nodded weakly. With that Trix Dawson whisked him off through the crowds. A television presenter stepped forward to question Spiky Mike, but Spiky Mike was staring after Dominic and ignored her completely.

Joanna was stunned. How could that have just happened? It was too unreal. The presenter was obviously trying to make sense of it all but Joanna was no longer listening. She couldn't take her eyes off a man in the crowd. She watched spellbound as the man slowly pulled off his beard, his moustache and wig. Just for an instant he stared straight at the camera. Straight at *her*, Joanna. Knowing she'd be watching.

'Marius King,' she whispered. 'I've just seen Marius King, *and he's coming for me!*'

# 25
## HIDDEN
## MEANINGS

'Are you sure you left your phone in here, Mr Hogan?' Isaac asked as he rummaged through the great pile of books on the library table for the third time.

'I'm pretty sure I had it in here last night,' replied the teacher, wheeling his chair round the table. 'I thought it would just turn up, but it hasn't – and I've been more interested in making sense of that manuscript than looking for the phone. I hope you didn't mind not watching the races on television this afternoon – it's just we so rarely get the opportunity to have the caves to ourselves without interruption.'

'I could check Vincent's study?' said Isaac helpfully.

'Would you mind? And drop off the manuscript whilst you're there. I'll see if I can find edited highlights of the racing on the news and then we can be up-to-date before the others return.'

Isaac left Mr Hogan flicking through the channels and hurried off to Vincent's study. The manuscript they'd been looking at should have been easy to translate, but they could make no sense of it – it was as though half the words were missing!

The manuscripts were kept on the top shelf of the bookcase. Isaac had to use a small wooden stepladder to reach it. As he did so he had a sudden memory of being a little boy and coming into Vincent's study and seeing Vincent standing on the steps. He must have only been about seven and thought Vincent was a giant. Vincent said he was looking for a special puzzle and wondered if Isaac liked puzzles too. When Isaac said yes, Vincent had gone to his desk and taken out two pieces of paper. Isaac had to work out a story by looking at the first word on one piece of paper and then the next word on the other. It had taken him all morning. Vincent had told him that in the olden days that was how people had kept special things secret . . .

Isaac stopped dead in his tracks – Why hadn't he thought of it before? The manuscript hadn't made sense because only half the words *were* there! There must be a second manuscript . . . All they needed to do was find it.

But that was easier said than done. Vincent's filing system had long been a mystery to Isaac and Mr Hogan. It seemed to be completely random yet his grandma had told him that Vincent had always been very particular in putting everything back in the right order. He would need to be methodical, not rush it. Wasn't that what Vincent had taught him?

Isaac looked round Vincent's study as if seeing it for the first time. What other secrets were hidden here? He went over to the fireplace and bent down. This was where Vincent must have made his silver fire and where his grandma had turned Excelsior's egg. What did it say in the old egg-turning manuscript?

*An egg placed in the dragon's breath for its final turning will be purified of all excess. The dragon born from such a flame will be sleek and fast, the perfect manifestation of physical flight.*

*Spiritus draconis.* Dragon's breath – the silver fire of alchemy. Perhaps Excelsior would make the fire to hatch out the new egg just as he had when Aurora was born. Isaac ran his hand over the great stone mantelpiece, his fingers suddenly tracing carved words he'd never noticed before: *ignem amore accende.*

He felt a quiver of excitement. *Light the fire with love.* Not a request but an order. An order for *him*? Isaac knelt down by the fireplace and closed his eyes. What did he love? Images flashed through his mind . . . his grandma . . . dragons . . . turning the dragon egg . . .

He felt it before he saw it.

The fire – its silver tongues of flame all around him, cradling him. Flames that leapt and twisted themselves into a crown of fire. Now the fire was all around him, encircling him, flooding over him and through him until he and the fire were one. It had a heat that didn't burn, but rather washed over him, cleansing him. Although it was strangely painful he didn't want it to stop. It made him feel happy . . . alive . . . It made him feel himself.

A soft buzzing noise from the sofa suddenly broke his thoughts. The fire went out in an instant. Isaac stood for a moment, dazed, before he realised that the buzzing was Mr Hogan's phone. It stopped as he picked it up. There were ten missed calls. All from Afra. Had something happened?

He heard a noise in the corridor outside and Mr Hogan calling, 'Isaac, are you there?'

'Yes,' called Isaac quickly. 'Sorry I took so long. I found your phone. Afra's been trying to call you.'

'I'm not surprised, come and see this – quickly! There's been a disaster at the Valentine Chase.'

'What?' said Isaac, aghast, following Mr Hogan back to the library.

'It's Joanna's friend Dominic. His dragon careered out of control and dropped down dead, but not before Spiky Mike had rescued him in spectacular fashion.'

They were transfixed by the televised replay of events until Mr Hogan's phone rang again.

'Afra!' said Mr Hogan answering the phone. 'Yes, we've seen. How is everyone? You should be back within the hour. Yes, Isaac's here. Do you want a word?'

Isaac took the phone. 'Hello, Afra. Yes of course I can get a scale bath ready. Is Aurora OK? Oh good. See you soon.' Isaac handed back the phone. His mind was in a whirl. *Dragons dropping dead at races; the missing manuscript; the silver fire . . .* He needed time to think.

Isaac turned to Mr Hogan. 'Why don't you go home? We can't do any more translating now. They'll need me to help and I've still got to turn the egg.'

'You're right,' said Mr Hogan. 'I'm best out of everyone's way. See you tomorrow.'

As soon as Aurora arrived back in her cave Isaac saw why the scale bath was necessary. The smooth shiny scales along her belly and back legs were encrusted with the stuff that Nemesis had spewed up.

'We cleaned her as best we could at the racecourse, but everything was so chaotic that in the end we decided to drive straight home,' said Afra, who was still visibly trembling.

Aurora was frantically scratching herself with her claws, raking the skin in an attempt to clean herself.

Hannibal was trying to help, but he was so distressed he was proving more of a hindrance.

'It won't come off,' he kept repeating over and over again.

'Isaac, will you help Mike clean her up?' said Afra quietly. 'I need to get Hannibal away before he completely breaks down.'

She went and gently touched Hannibal's shoulder. 'Hannibal, let Mike and Isaac do this. We'll go and get something ready for her to eat.'

Hannibal looked up.

'She won't talk to me,' he said sadly. 'I don't know what to do.' He stood up and allowed Afra to lead him out of the cave as if he were a little boy.

'We'll need gloves and brushes for this, it's disgusting,' grimaced Spiky Mike. 'And pass me that specimen jar. I want to send some of this muck off to a private lab to get it tested.'

Isaac looked in disgust at the grey gunge. 'Won't the WDRF be doing the same?' he asked.

'You bet,' said Spiky Mike. 'But what makes you think they'll tell the rest of us – they'll want to play down this incident as much as they can.'

Isaac went to stroke Aurora. 'Hey, girl, I saw you on the news, you were amazing rescuing Dominic like that. So were you, Spiky Mike. I didn't know you could fly like that – I thought you never flew?'

'Needs must,' said Spiky Mike gruffly, scrubbing hard at the scales with a metal-bristled brush. 'Can you rub this oil where I've cleaned her belly, Isaac?'

They worked in silence until at last Aurora was silver and shining and bright. She was calm again, but very subdued. They'd just finished clearing up when Spiky Mike's phone rang.

'Giovanni?' he said. 'Yeah, we're back from the races. We've just finished cleaning up Aurora. Afra's looking after Hannibal. He's very distressed. Everything all right in Wales?' he added in an offhand way that Isaac didn't believe for a moment.

Giovanni's reply made Spiky Mike frown. 'I'm not surprised you said you didn't believe her. The man's in –'

The phone conversation was suddenly interrupted by Afra bursting into the cave.

'Mike!' She was out of breath with running. 'The WDRF have just phoned. Marius King's escaped from prison!'

Spiky Mike looked in disbelief. 'Giovanni, did you catch that? Am I concerned? Very! In fact I'm coming up straightaway. Expect me very late. Look, you may think I'm being melodramatic but can you put Excelsior up in the top cave tonight?'

Spiky Mike put his phone back in his pocket and looked grimly at his two colleagues. 'It's too much of a coincidence, Marius King escaping from jail only to turn up at a race where a dragon dies in such spectacular fashion.'

'And now you think Marius King will go after Joanna?' asked Afra in alarm.

'It's common knowledge where she is. I can't take the risk,' was Spiky Mike's immediate response.

Afra knew he was right. For all they knew Marius King could be speeding up the motorway to Wales as they spoke.

'Be careful yourself,' she said kissing her boyfriend goodbye. 'And don't worry about us – Isaac will help me.'

Spiky Mike picked up his jacket and was gone.

# 26
## A SAFE PLACE
# TO STAY?

Spiky Mike arrived in the early hours of the morning, unshaven and exhausted.

'Are you sure you need to take Excelsior back to London?' Giovanni asked, concerned at the state of his friend.

Spiky Mike was adamant. 'You're too isolated. At least in Brixton we'll be able to keep a tight watch on who comes in and out of the caves.'

'And Joanna?'

'What about me?' yawned a sleepy Joanna, appearing in the doorway in her dressing gown. 'It *was* Marius King that I saw, wasn't it? That's why you're here. You won't let him hurt Excelsior?'

'Hi, Jo. Why do you think I drove through the night?' said Spiky Mike more gently than she expected. 'I'm afraid it was Marius King and

I'm going to keep you safely out of his reach until he's caught. Now go back to bed. Before you argue, I need you to be ready to go home tomorrow – or later this morning I should say.'

'I'm not going to argue – I just wanted to say thank you for coming.' Joanna said.

By eleven o'clock Spiky Mike and Joanna were driving back down the motorway in one of Giovanni's vans. Theirs still had to be decontaminated after carrying Aurora back from the race. Already the winter beauty of Snowdonia had given way to a ten-mile traffic jam. In the end they pulled into a motorway café and ate part of the picnic lunch Lucia had packed for them. They hadn't spoken much during the drive, limiting their conversation to Joanna and Excelsior's flying excursions around the mountain, but Joanna couldn't bear it a minute longer.

'Spiky Mike, what do you think Marius King's going to do next?'

'I don't know,' said Spiky Mike. 'But I'd like to know the connection between his appearance at the Valentine Chase and what happened to Nemesis.'

'Dominic looked terrible yesterday,' said Joanna, hoping Spiky Mike wouldn't make any caustic comments about boyfriends.

He didn't. He just nodded.

'Spiky Mike,' Joanna began tentatively, knowing that in bringing up the subject she was reopening the can of worms that had caused him to walk out of the caves. 'You know those raised weals I found on Excelsior's neck and how they disappeared . . .'

'Yes . . .' said Spiky Mike equally cautiously.

'Isaac thought they could be an allergic reaction. He looked it up. I think they were made by something on the scarf Dominic lent me. The thing is, Dominic didn't want me to borrow the scarf – it was his trainer who insisted I wore it.'

Before Spiky Mike could make any comment, his phone rang.

'Afra!' His face softened into a smile. 'We're stuck in traffic . . . Afra, what's the matter? Why are you crying?'

Joanna saw a look of horror flash across Spiky Mike's face. She sat still as stone, trying to hear what was going on. Spiky Mike had gone as white as a sheet. He'd closed his eyes but he was still listening. Listening about some terrible thing. He kept shaking his head. What was it? What had happened?

'Oh, please may it not be Agnes,' Joanna kept whispering to herself over and over. 'Not Agnes.'

When Spiky Mike finally put down his phone, he just sat there staring out through the window.

'Spiky Mike?' Joanna had to swallow hard, but not knowing was worse than anything. 'What's happened? Tell me.' Her voice grew loud. '*Please tell me.*'

'It's Aurora . . .' Spiky Mike was so choked up he could barely speak. 'Her fire . . . Jo . . . Afra said she was so brave . . . but her fire . . . it just went out . . . she's dead!'

'No!' screamed Joanna. 'NO! She *can't* be! You're lying!' Joanna flung open the van door and tried to jump out into the motorway car park. She had to get away from such lies. She'd go back to Wales. She'd . . .

But Spiky Mike grabbed her arm and pulled her back.

'*OK*! Let's go home then. *Drive*! DRIVE!' screamed Joanna.

Spiky Mike didn't move. 'Listen, Joanna. Listen to me! We can't go back to Brixton. Whatever killed Nemesis killed Aurora too so it must be really, really contagious.'

'Where shall we go?'

'I don't know.' Spiky Mike looked dazed. 'I'm thinking.'

For a while neither of them spoke or even moved. Then suddenly Spiky Mike turned the key in the ignition and started the engine.

'Are we going back to Wales?' sobbed Joanna, trying hard to control her tears and failing.

'We can't,' said Spiky Mike. 'That's where Marius King thinks you are. I've got to take you somewhere safe.'

'Safe for Excelsior too?' asked Joanna terrified by his words.

'We'll go to the only place I know where there are empty dragon caves,' came the reply. 'The only place we *can* go is Brighton.'

Joanna felt sick in the pit of her stomach. Not Brighton! Not to the caves where Vincent died – Marius King's own caves! She didn't dare say anything to Spiky Mike. His grim face stared straight out at the road as they sped along the motorway, every minute bringing them closer and closer to her worst nightmare.

Joanna called her father and they made one stop at a service station, to meet up with Anthony Morris, who was anxious to see his daughter before she went into hiding. He had alarming news for them.

'Apparently Nemesis and Aurora died of a new and virulent form of dragon influenza. I'm afraid three other dragons from the Valentine Chase are also dead.'

'No news of Marius King, I suppose,' said Spiky Mike.

'Nothing more. I've also been asked to tell you that the WDRF have arranged police protection for Joanna in the caves, for as long as it's needed. An undercover detective, Leonie Reese, will meet you in Brighton.'

'What?' said Joanna aghast. 'I don't need police protection!'

'It's that or you come back home with me,' said her father sternly.

'I'm not leaving Excelsior for one minute!' protested Joanna loudly.

'So try and be a little grown up about this,' Anthony Morris was trying hard not to lose his patience.

'I am being grown up about it,' protested Joanna indignantly.

'Then stop drawing attention to yourself by yelling so loudly.'

'I don't think Marius King's got spies out here, Dad,' said Joanna.

'I was thinking of the press, young lady. We've had a score of journalists wanting to know your whereabouts. We've managed to get a news blackout so far because you're still a minor but I'm sure any freelance paparazzi would be delighted to photograph you shouting at a motorway service station. I wish poor Hannibal could have the same protection as you. The poor man's distraught, yet at every turn there's journalists waiting for him. We're arranging for him to fly home to the States first thing tomorrow.'

Hannibal! Up till then Joanna hadn't allowed

herself to even try and imagine what Hannibal must be feeling, or Afra. Just the thought of them made her burst into tears again. 'I'm sorry, Dad . . . tell Hannibal . . . and . . . Afra . . . I . . . I . . .' But the words just wouldn't come.

Anthony Morris put his arms around his daughter and hugged her tightly.

'I'll give them both your love and say that you're thinking of them just as I know they're thinking of you. Mum and Aaron send you lots of love too. We'll be thinking of you all the time. All I ask is that you do what Spiky Mike and Detective Reese tell you.'

The Royal Brighton Pavilion was glowing and majestic in the early evening light, but Spiky Mike and Joanna ignored the exotic beauty of the domes and turrets – they were too busy looking out for DC Reese. She was waiting at the entrance of the dragon loading bays.

'Hello,' she smiled climbing up into the cab. 'DC Leonie Reese, good to meet you. Let's go and park this van and then I can show you where you'll be staying. Luckily for us two port-a-cabins were left down here after the builders finished clearing the caves.'

'What about Excelsior, DC Reese?' asked Joanna.

'Call me Leonie. Take your pick of all the caves. You'll know best – I wasn't quite sure what . . .

Excelsior needed.' She peered nervously into the back of the van. 'I haven't actually come across a real dragon before. My boyfriend is very keen on watching the races though. In fact he saw you win at New Year.'

Spiky Mike drove the van slowly down into the caves to a large parking bay just off the central hall.

'Here we are. Do you want to tell Excelsior why we're here or shall I do it?' he asked Joanna.

Joanna looked into the back of the van where Excelsior was beginning to stir. 'I'll do it, but he's going to be very upset and I'm not sure how he'll react. Please will you stay with me?'

Spiky Mike turned to DC Reese. 'Would you mind if we just have a few minutes in private?'

'Of course,' she agreed. 'I'll go and put the kettle on.'

Excelsior was wide awake and itching to get out of the van. Before they could stop him he was down the ramp looking around in confusion.

'Brighton? Why have you brought me to Brighton?'

'Mind-blend, tell him in a mind-blend,' insisted Spiky Mike. 'And, Jo, you've *got* to take control.'

When she told him about Aurora, Excelsior's grief was beyond measure. His anguished howls echoed around the limestone caves and erupted as great blasts of fire and smoke into the air. But somehow Joanna held him in his torment. Her own small tears told her dragon that she knew and understood. She entered the fire whirling inside him and, just as it was when they fireballed, she found the still quiet space at the centre and waited until his great anger and pain subsided into sadness.

Slowly, slowly, as Excelsior grew calm, Joanna relaxed her control until finally she slipped off his back. She stroked the silver scales of his neck.

'I love you, XL,' she whispered. 'And I will do everything I can to keep you safe.'

Excelsior allowed Joanna and Spiky Mike to lead him to his cave.

'I'm OK,' he whispered to Joanna. 'I just need time on my own.' Joanna reluctantly left him and followed Spiky Mike back to the central hall where the two port-a-cabins looked rather out of place.

'I don't remember any of this,' said Joanna, looking round in surprise at the bare rock of the walls. 'Last year everything was all metal and shiny tiles.'

'These are the original caves much as they were when they were excavated at the beginning of the nineteenth century,' said Spiky Mike. 'This is what survived the explosion.'

'Have you ever visited the Pavilion?' Leonie asked coming to join them with two very welcome cups of tea. 'They have dragon wallpaper!'

Joanna tried to smile as she sipped her hot tea. She

knew Leonie was trying to be kind, but nothing she could say was going to make her feel any better.

'Let's just be thankful that, for tonight, Excelsior is safe and so are you!' said Spiky Mike. 'Now I'm bushwhacked after all that driving so if everyone doesn't mind I'm suggesting something to eat and an early night.'

'I've put a couple of pizzas in the oven already,' said Leonie. 'They should be just about done.'

After supper Spiky Mike quickly disappeared and Joanna said she would get some rest too. She sat down on the bed. It seemed quite comfy, although she didn't know how much she would sleep. This morning she'd woken to Welsh clouds and mountains and now she was in a port-a-cabin in a cave in Brighton!

'I wonder how long we'll be here for?' she sighed as she turned off her bedside lamp.

# 27
## A DREAM
# MOMENT

Joanna woke abruptly, wondering where she was. But how could she forget? She was in Brighton hiding from Marius King. And Aurora was dead!

Joanna still couldn't believe it was true as she lay there unable to get back to sleep. Everything was silent except for the tick of a clock on the wall. She wished she hadn't noticed that. Now she'd spend the rest of the night listening to the ticking -- and all the thoughts rattling round her head that wouldn't silence themselves! She switched on her bedside lamp. Three o'clock.

Joanna got out of bed. She knew why she couldn't sleep. Something was niggling her at the back of her brain; some connection that she wasn't making about this whole situation. She wondered if Excelsior was awake too. Perhaps talking to him would help.

She quickly threw on a tracksuit, picked up a torch and slipped out of her room.

The light shone slowly around the hewn rock walls of the enormous cave of the central hall. This was where Excelsior had fought and killed Prometheus and where Marius King had sworn to her that he would exact his revenge. She shivered quickly and hurried past Spiky Mike's port-a-cabin into the tunnel that led to Excelsior's cave. At the end of it she thought she saw the flash of a torch. Spiky Mike can't have been able to sleep either and had gone to check on Excelsior.

'Spiky Mike,' she called down the passageway. 'Are you there?' The light seemed to flash back at Joanna before it quickly disappeared into the cave.

'Spiky Mike?' she called again. 'It's me, Joanna!'

Even as she ran down the tunnel she knew something was wrong. Spiky Mike would have replied, even if it was to tell her to go back to bed. Who was it?

She tried calling to Excelsior in her mind but he did not reply. Should she turn back? But that would mean leaving her dragon to face whoever it was alone. She had to find out who was in the cave. Turning off her torch she made her way silently in the dark to the end of the tunnel. The cave lay just to her left. Then she heard them.

A man laughing.

A woman shouting.

And a boy crying.

She recognised two of them. Marius King and Trix Dawson. Was the boy Dominic Pieterson?

*But how did they know we were here?* wondered Joanna. And then it dawned on her. *They were hiding in the caves too . . .*

Suddenly it all fell into place. Marius King was behind everything; the sickness, the cheating . . . and now he was about to avenge himself on Excelsior!

*XL! XL!* She sent her thoughts into the cave, desperate for some sort of reply from her dragon. But there was nothing, just a blank silence. She peeped quickly round the side of the cave.

Spiky Mike had left two large lanterns ready for the morning. They were now alight and casting strange and monstrous shadows on the wall. Marius King was talking to Trix. Luckily they had their backs to the entrance. Where was Dominic? She had to look hard. There he was, leaning against the cave wall, trying to keep in the shadows.

Excelsior, his silver body coiled and helpless, lay on the far side of the cave. She could see his eyelids twitching every now and then and a thin wisp of smoke from his nostril told her he was breathing.

'He's alive!' she repeated to herself over and over

again, eyes shut in relief. She could feel her heart banging silently against the wall of her chest and her legs were shaking. She had to go back, she had to go and get Spiky Mike. Joanna opened her eyes and . . .

Too late! A strong arm grabbed hold of her and pulled her into the cave. In the flash of torchlight she saw cold blue eyes glittering in triumph.

'At last! Ms Joanna Morris – our little World Champion!' sneered Marius King. 'How I have dreamed of this. There was I planning a little journey to Wales, but instead you've made everything easy for me by turning up at my caves *so* conveniently!'

'What have you done to Excelsior?' Joanna managed to stammer, unable to take her eyes off her dragon. 'If you've hurt him . . . I'll . . .'

Marius King gave a low silky laugh. 'What? Kill me! I don't think so. As for your dragon . . .' Marius King threw a contemptuous glance at the inert silver body. 'He was uncooperative so we knocked him out cold with a sedative dart. Don't worry, by the time he comes round it will all be over. Why not come and see?'

Joanna rushed to Excelsior's side and tried to wake him to no avail. 'What do you mean *it will all be over*? What will be over?'

'Dear sister,' said Marius King, turning to Trix

Dawson with a wave of his hand. 'Why don't you explain. I find all the technical details so boring.'

'Your *sister?*' said Joanna aghast, looking from Marius King to Trix Dawson. They looked nothing like each other – except for the hatred in their eyes.

'Ah, she's looking to see if there's a family resemblance!' said Marius King mockingly. 'Let me see – we both love money, power, oh and what was that final one? Oh yes, we both share an intense desire to bring down the world of dragon racing and *you* in particular.'

'Marius, let Dominic tell her what's going to happen to her dragon,' laughed Trix spitefully. 'She's got a bit of a crush on him.' Trix turned to Dominic. 'Tell her what happened to *your* dragon after his little injection.'

Dominic snarled and tried to kick out at Trix, but he couldn't. Joanna saw that his hands and feet were tied with rope. Trix pushed him, cracking his head against the cave wall. He staggered and fell onto the floor.

Trix looked on dispassionately. 'Dominic, you disappoint me. But then you've disappointed me all season! Your total lack of co-operation isn't helping your nan at all. Carol's going to be so disappointed when she finds out how you've let me down.'

'You might have killed my dragon,' he shouted wildly. 'But if you hurt my nan I'll . . .'

Trix kicked him sharply. 'I don't think you're in a position to do anything.'

Joanna felt sick. She could see blood on Dominic's face. Instinctively she looked towards the cave entrance. Why hadn't she gone back to get Spiky Mike when she could? Marius King saw her glance and laughed.

'Would you *really* want to leave your dragon at such a moment as this, Ms Morris? Now, sister, it's time to *show* our dear friend exactly what you did to Nemesis . . .'

Trix Dawson snapped open a small metal case and took out a syringe. She held it up so that Joanna could see it contained a dark-green liquid.

'This,' she said sharply, 'is a new strain of dragon flu – HN23/7 – highly contagious with a ninety-nine per cent mortality rate. The first symptoms are thick phlegm forming in a dragon's lungs. Normally a dragon would use its own fire to evaporate it, only with this particular strain of virus a dragon's fire is first weakened and then extinguished. Once this happens the dragon starts to drown in its own phlegm. But what finally kills the dragon is not the extinguishing of the fire or the suffocation – it's the despair it feels as its life force drains away!'

Joanna felt the bile in her stomach heave. She was going to be sick, violently sick. She staggered to her feet and spat out the foul liquid from her mouth over the cave floor.

'You are evil,' she spluttered. 'Evil! *I hate you!*' She threw herself against Marius King and battered him again and again with her fists. 'I HAAAATE YOU!'

Marius King pushed her easily away, as if removing something unpleasant.

'Just as I hate you,' he hissed. 'Now, just as I lost everything because of you, so you too will lose everything!'

He suddenly grabbed hold of her and pinned her arms against her body so that she couldn't move.

'Trix,' he ordered in a hard cold voice. 'Inject Excelsior with the virus.'

Trix slid down beside Excelsior and gently cradled his head in her lap. It seemed such a gentle tender thing to do that Joanna wondered if perhaps she was going to refuse.

Then Trix expertly pushed Excelsior's head upwards to reveal his throat. Joanna had never noticed before how translucent the skin was there. It seemed to glow with fiery brightness.

'A dragon creates fire in a special fire chamber,' said Trix matter-of-factly, as if she was a teacher in a lesson, 'which it exhales through its mouth via its windpipe. This point here, which you can see glowing, is where the fire passes from the windpipe into the dragon's mouth. It is the most vulnerable part of a dragon because here the skin is thinnest, allowing me to inject the dragon . . . so.'

Trix Dawson picked up the syringe and pressed it against Excelsior's throat. Joanna tried to tear herself free from Marius King to fling herself at Trix Dawson. But Marius King was far too strong and held her fast.

Joanna closed her eyes. She couldn't watch. She felt her legs buckle underneath her and heard her own screams. It was all too late. Trix Dawson stood up. In her hand was the empty syringe.

Marius King dropped Joanna onto the floor, letting her scrabble as best she could over to Excelsior's still unconscious body. His work here was done; his revenge complete. Without a backward glance he walked out of the cave.

Trix Dawson turned briefly to Joanna.

'Give this letter to the WDRF. If my demands are met I will release the formula for the anti-viral medication. But you'll have to hurry. By my reckoning your dragon has got six hours max before it's bye bye, Excelsior. Even so, the WDRF will find it invaluable as the flu epidemic sweeps through the dragon world.'

She dropped the letter beside Joanna.

'Now, what to do with your *boyfriend*?' Trix barely

looked at the blood-stained Dominic huddled against the cave wall. 'I would hate to spoil a blossoming teenage romance, so I'll leave him with you.' Trix blew each of them a kiss and followed her brother out of the cave.

But Joanna didn't even know they had gone. She was lost in a world of heartbreak and pain. Her beautiful, shiny, beloved silver dragon was dying! How could she live without him?

'XL! XL!' she sobbed. Her voice echoed forlornly round the cave, but her dragon could not hear her.

## 28
### GOING
# HOME

'Jo! Joanna!'

Through a haze of anguish and tears Joanna was suddenly aware of someone close by calling her name and kicking her away from Excelsior.

She grabbed tighter hold of the scaled body.

'I won't leave you, XL,' she cried. 'They can't make me leave you now.'

Suddenly two feet pushed her so hard that she was forced to let go, winded by the blow.

'JOANNA!' A blood-stained pale face with dark-ringed eyes was peering at her through a shock of black hair.

'Dominic!' Joanna screamed. 'Leave me alone!' She flung herself back against Excelsior's unconscious body.

'I'll kick you away again if you don't listen to me,'

threatened Dominic, shuffling closer, his arms and legs still tightly tied.

'Why should I?' said Joanna sullenly. 'My dragon is dying.'

'If that's what you want, go ahead, mope and cry. But he's not dead yet,' said Dominic. 'We can help him. Now untie me, quick!'

Joanna looked at him uncertainly.

'Jo, come *on*! You're wasting precious seconds. Didn't you hear what Trix said? She's got a formula for anti-viral medication.'

'So?' snivelled Joanna looking at Dominic blankly.

'Jo, sometimes you are so stupid – the anti-virals are the one thing that can save Excelsior. Now untie this rope.'

Joanna didn't need telling again. As soon as he was free Dominic took Joanna's hand and started pulling her out of the cave.

Joanna, though, resisted. 'We can't leave Excelsior,' she cried pulling her hand away.

Dominic waved Trix's envelope in front of her face.

'This is what will save Excelsior. So come on.' He pulled the still reluctant Joanna down the passage. 'Come on, we've got to wake up Spiky Mike! Jump on him! Throw cold water on him! Anything! We've got to wake him up so that we can get Trix's demands to the WDRF.'

Joanna had to really shake Spiky Mike he was in such a dead sleep.

'It's Marius King,' she yelled. 'He was hiding here too! And Trix Dawson is his sister and she's injected Excelsior. Just get up, *please*!' She half pulled half pushed Spiky Mike down the tunnel to the unconscious dragon. Just one look at Excelsior and he was wide awake.

Immediately he sent Joanna to run and wake Leonie to radio for help. Dominic went too. He was desperate for someone to rescue his nan, who had been locked up in one of her own dragon caves for days.

'I'll radio them to send a team immediately, Dominic,' said Leonie calmly. 'I need to look at your cut too, it might need stitches.'

Dominic shook his head. 'I'm fine – it looks worse than it is. I'm much more worried about my nan.'

'What about Trix's letter? What about the anti-viral formula?' demanded Joanna impatiently. 'Show her the letter, Dominic.'

Leonie carefully read the letter.

'Joanna,' she said slowly, 'we always have to think very carefully about whether or not we comply with the terms of a ransom note. And her demands are nearly impossible.'

'What does she want?' asked Spiky Mike, who'd come to find out what was going on.

Leonie handed him the letter. He read it aloud so that they could all hear.

'*Two million pounds* – thought it'd be more than that. *Immunity for Marius King* – obviously! *And Vincent Marlowe's papers and manuscripts* – the surprise twist of the knife. Not a lot then!' he added sarcastically. 'And in return we get a formula which may or may not make the anti-viral medication needed to treat dragon flu.'

Joanna looked at him fearfully. 'If we don't do as they ask, then Excelsior will die!'

He looked at his young flyer and shook his head.

'Jo,' he swallowed hard. 'Even if we decide to go along with these demands it may not be possible to get everything sorted in time.'

'Money!' exclaimed Joanna. 'I've got money – all the money I've earned. Plus Vincent left me a whole load for when I'm older. We can use that. And all his papers and manuscripts – they're mine I can do with them what I want!' She looked at Spiky Mike desperately. 'Please, I'll do anything to save Excelsior, *please*!'

Spiky Mike looked grimly at Leonie. 'You heard her. We've got to at least try. Tell the WDRF and your boss that we want to go along with the demands.'

She nodded. 'I'll do my best. But Marius King's immunity is out of my hands. Come with me,

Dominic, you might have valuable information that will help us.'

'In the meantime, Jo,' said Spiky Mike, 'let's see what we can do for Excelsior.'

They returned to the cave and Spiky Mike immediately began to vigorously shake the dragon's unconscious body. 'Come on, boy, we need you to wake up.'

Excelsior twitched but stayed asleep. Spiky Mike turned to Joanna. 'If you try and wake him up with a mind-blend, I'll rouse him physically. We need to keep him active for as long as possible. And there are certain massage techniques we can use to stimulate his lungs to get him to cough up as much phlegm as we can manage. But I warn you, it's not going to be pretty.'

Joanna nodded and started to try and mind-blend with Excelsior as Spiky Mike shook and rubbed and pushed at the dragon to wake him up.

Suddenly Excelsior gave a great shudder and to their relief he opened his eyes.

'XL!' shouted Joanna. 'Oh thank goodness you've woken up,'

Excelsior looked wildly around him and managed to stand.

'Marius King was here,' he groaned. 'He shot me with something – JoJo, I feel terrible.' Excelsior suddenly started to splutter and cough. 'JoJo, I can't breathe properly,' he rasped. 'What's happening?'

Joanna looked on horrified. It couldn't be happening this fast, could it?

Spiky Mike didn't wait but started frantically rubbing backwards and forwards along Excelsior's sides to try and stimulate Excelsior's breathing.

'Jo,' he called urgently. 'Go into the mind-blend again and support Excelsior as he makes a fireball. Get him to make it as hot and as fast as possible and see if we can get rid of some of the muck in his lungs.'

Joanna knew that as soon as she mind-blended with Excelsior it would be impossible to hide the truth from him. To her surprise he was a great deal calmer about it than she was. He understood immediately the need to spin the fire in his belly to get as much power from it as possible. It was hard work, but slowly, slowly the fire began to move. She could sense Excelsior's breathing become easier. She breathed her own sigh of relief. If he could keep this up it would give them some extra time.

'JoJo?' said XL slowly. 'Will you ask Spiky Mike to take us home to Brixton? If . . . if I'm going to . . .' He didn't finish his sentence. Joanna wouldn't let him.

'XL you're going to get better! See the fire is already helping you . . .'

'JoJo, I just want to go home,' was Excelsior's only reply.

DC Reese returned to the cave entrance.

'I'm afraid your president, Sir John Miller, has refused point blank to comply with any of Trix Dawson's demands. He's says they can't be seen giving in to blackmail. They're sending an emergency medical team down immediately. The caves are now officially in quarantine. No one is to leave.'

And then Spiky Mike said something that made Joanna realise that he really was the best trainer ever.

'I'm not prepared to wait around for a bunch of incompetent medics to kill our dragon so I'm going to ignore that quarantine order.'

He turned to Joanna. 'Joanna, I may not be able to do anything about Trix's demands, but I'm damned if that stupid president is going to stop us helping Excelsior. So if that dragon wants to go back home to Brixton, then to Brixton we will go.'

Joanna ran and hugged her trainer. 'Thank you, thank you!' she cried.

'You won't stop them or report them, will you, Leonie?' said Dominic standing forgotten behind her.

'No!' said Leonie. 'In fact I'm going to radio in for a police escort . . .'

Spiky Mike didn't wait to hear the rest. 'I'll get the van ready.'

Joanna went and stroked Excelsior, who was concentrating hard on spinning the fire.

'Did you hear that, XL?' she whispered. 'We're going home!'

# 29
## AD ASTRA
# PER ASPERA

Even with the police escort whisking them through the early rush-hour traffic Joanna thought it was taking forever to get back to Brixton. Before they left, Spiky Mike had shown her how to massage Excelsior's sides to help him cough up any phlegm. He stopped and smiled at her. 'Pretend you're me – get really cross and make him spin the fire.'

Joanna couldn't speak. It was too much to bear to see Excelsior lying there so helpless, wracked by the rasping cough, gasping for breath and spewing out this disgusting filth; a mixture of dark fire, thick smoke and sticky phlegm. Spiky Mike was just about to shut the door of the van when suddenly Dominic pushed his way through and suddenly kissed Joanna on her cheek as if to say, 'If anyone can do this, you can!'

Before Joanna could reply he'd disappeared and the van door shut behind him. Spiky Mike started the engine and they were away.

Now here they were speeding along, yet it wasn't fast enough. What made matters worse was that every bump and turn seemed to set Excelsior off into a paroxysm of coughing and spluttering.

Despite being exhausted, Joanna continued to rub his sides for all she was worth.

'But I don't think I'm doing any good,' she cried. 'You *must* spin the fire, XL, SPIN!'

Excelsior gave another rasping cough, and this time Joanna noticed there was no fire with the phlegm, just sticky black smoke.

'Oh, JoJo, I can't do this, it's too hard. Please just let me fall asleep . . .'

Joanna softly stroked her dragon's neck.

'Hey, Excelsior,' she whispered. 'That's what I said to you the last time we travelled back together from Brighton. But you wouldn't let me fall asleep. You wouldn't let me give up. Instead you held me safe and you showed me how Vincent's silver fire is found in everything, holding it together, making all things new, all things whole. It's why we're here and it's just a touch away. It's love! It's life! All the things that make you, you! Oh, XL, you made it when Aurora was born, so now make it for yourself.' She wept uncontrollably.

'*Please* make it for yourself.'

'I can't,' said Excelsior quietly. 'Not for myself, you *know* it doesn't work like that.'

'Can *I* make it for you? Show me! Show me how,' pleaded Joanna.

But Excelsior didn't answer for suddenly he began to shake and tremble, his body was convulsing and twisting, forcing Joanna to leap out of the way. She had to watch helplessly until he fell completely still. She crept slowly forward.

'Please don't be dead, please don't . . .' To her relief he coughed out a great snort of thick black smoke. His eyes opened, then immediately closed.

'Spiky Mike,' called Joanna frantically banging on the glass partition that separated them. 'Please hurry up, he's worse than ever!'

'We're nearly there – five minutes tops,' Spiky Mike called back. 'We're just at the top of Brixton Hill.'

Joanna laid her cheek against the dragon, frantically rubbing Excelsior's sides for all she was worth. Before she knew it she had entered a mind-blend. But this mind-blend was different! It was like being lost in a black fog. She knew Excelsior was there, somewhere, but all the time he was drifting further away from her . . . there was no fire in his belly to spin. If only she could just touch the silver fire that lived within – that *was* – her dragon. Then, before she could stop him,

Excelsior began to slip out of the mind-blend.

'XL, XL,' she sobbed. 'Don't go! Don't leave me.' She reached out to hold him.

'Let me go, JoJo!' sobbed a voice she barely recognised. 'It's too late. There is no more fire. I can't stand it any more; not this darkness, this cold, this despair.'

'I love you, XL,' cried Joanna. 'I've always loved you! Ever since I saw you crawling down the clock tower at the town hall. Do you remember?' She thought of him as he'd been then, just a tiny flicker of silver . . .

She stopped. She could see silver now in the darkness, or was it just her imagination playing tricks? No, it was there . . . she could see a tiny flame of silver.

'XL,' she shouted. 'XL, look!' Suddenly she could feel Excelsior in the mind-blend again.

'*Spiritus draconis*,' he rasped. 'Dragon's Breath!'

They could both see a figure walking towards them very slowly, although he was still a long way away.

'Who is it?' asked Joanna curiously.

'The Alchemist, of course,' sighed Excelsior. 'He's come to take me home.'

Suddenly Joanna was aware that the van had stopped and the doors had opened, but she didn't break the mind-blend, not even when they hoisted Excelsior onto a stretcher to take him to his cave.

Steadfastly she stayed by her dragon's side, watching as the Alchemist walked ever closer bringing with him the silver fire.

They were in Excelsior's own cave and there were strong and willing hands to rub the sides of the dragon. They took it in turns; regardless of the early hour, of tiredness, of their own grief – Spiky Mike, Afra and Hannibal, who had refused to catch his flight home. Even without looking, Joanna could tell who was massaging Excelsior at any particular time. Spiky Mike was brusque but thorough in contrast to Afra who was careful and soothing, then Hannibal, physically powerful and insistent – each one willing Excelsior to stay alive. And all the time Joanna could feel Excelsior's growing excitement.

'I haven't seen the Alchemist for such a long time,' he chattered, just like his normal self. 'It will be like old times. I'll just go and get him, JoJo. Stay there.'

Joanna felt Excelsior pull away from her. She knew she should be happy for him. He was going to the light, to be with Vincent . . .

But how could she live without him? Oh how could she bear this pain? She could feel the warmth of the fire now and the silver light was growing stronger. Excelsior must have found Vincent. This was it, her last chance to say goodbye. The light was growing so bright that it was overwhelming her.

'Goodbye, XL,' she whispered. 'I love you . . .'

'You need to let go now, Joanna,' said a voice close by. 'I've got him. He'll be quite safe.'

Breaking that mind-blend was the hardest thing she had ever done, but she did it – and for a brief second Joanna saw the Alchemist. Only he wasn't as she remembered him. He was smaller, younger . . . It wasn't Vincent at all.

'No!' she cried. 'Not you? It *can't* be you!'

# 30
## THE
## ALCHEMIST

'*Isaac?*' Joanna sat there stunned. How could Isaac be the Alchemist! That was impossible! What did it mean? She desperately wanted to go back into the mind-blend again to see if it really had been him but she couldn't. It was too late for that now because she'd never mind-blend with Excelsior again! The reality was too much for her.

'XL, XL!' she wailed. Desperately she touched his body, feeling the solidity of his great muscles, the silky sheen of his scales. He was so still, so peaceful. Like he was asleep.

Suddenly she sat up as the truth struck her like a thunderbolt. She put her hand on his belly and felt it rise in that slow wonderful rise of ordinary breathing! And it was *warm*. Her dragon, her beautiful wonderful Excelsior was alive!

She turned round to look at the others. They were standing there in watchful silence.

'Where is Isaac?' asked Joanna, aware that her voice was quivering with emotion.

'In Vincent's study with Mr Hogan. They've been working there all night,' said Afra. 'Why? Joanna, what's happened? We suddenly saw this silver light flash through Excelsior . . .'

'It's alchemy!' said Joanna. 'I saw the Alchemist in the mind-blend . . . I thought it was Vincent coming to take Excelsior, but it wasn't – it was Isaac!'

The three of them stared at her in astonishment. Hannibal raised his eyebrows.

'Isaac? So he and Mr Hogan must have made sense of Vincent's manuscripts.

'Yes, indeed we have!' A triumphant Mr Hogan wheeled his chair into the cave. 'But before we tell you everything, our young Alchemist here has an important job to complete if he is to save Excelsior.' He spun his chair over to the side and Isaac walked slowly into the room. In his hand he carried a small beaker of pale-gold liquid.

Now it was Afra's turn to cry out. 'I remember that pale gold – *aqua regia* – the elixir of life. It's what Vincent gave you, Joanna, when he saved your life.'

'I couldn't have made it without Mr Hogan's help.

He explained how to follow the chemical formula, I just made the fire,' said Isaac modestly.

Joanna jumped out of the way. She watched mesmerised as Isaac gently woke Excelsior and poured the liquid into his mouth.

'That's it, XL, go back to sleep again,' he whispered.

'Go back to sleep!' Excelsior suddenly sat up. 'I don't need to sleep! In fact I'm starving – a bucket of chicken livers is what I'd really like!'

After that everyone was talking and laughing and Joanna ran forward and hugged and kissed her dragon. Oh she was so happy!

She looked around for Isaac. What on earth could she say to thank him? He was standing talking to Spiky Mike, who was shaking his hand and patting him on the back, and Afra had given him a hug and Hannibal kept saying, 'Man that was something else.'

She walked slowly over. 'Isaac . . . I . . .'

'It's fine, Joanna, glad I could help,' said Isaac quickly and he turned away to go and talk to Mr Hogan.

'I'll get Excelsior's chicken livers,' said Joanna hastily.

She took her time on purpose but when she came back Joanna was surprised to see only Hannibal in the cave. He was talking quietly to Excelsior. She guessed they were talking about Aurora. Tears filled her eyes. How could Hannibal bear it? To see Excelsior alive when yesterday – *just yesterday!*

– Aurora had died of the same terrible virus. She was just going to put the bucket down and leave when Hannibal called to her.

'Isaac tried to save Aurora too – but he didn't know how. Those few hours before Aurora died he ransacked Vincent's study, trying to find some list he needed that would tell him which manuscripts to use. It was there all the time with Isaac's name on, just waiting for him in the top drawer. It was signed *To my apprentice* so I guess Vincent recognised Isaac had the ability to do these things even then.'

Joanna didn't know what to say. She stood next to her dearest rival just letting him talk.

'Aurora was such a beautiful dragon, better than I deserved. She was so different from Prometheus. She really cared! About everything. And she was always learning – always pestering Excelsior to give away your racing secrets! Now she's gone I wonder what I shall do. Perhaps I should go back home to the States and race there – fewer memories.'

He patted Excelsior again. 'Hey, champ,' he smiled sadly, 'I'll beat you and Jo in a race yet – some day! In the meantime perhaps you'd like something to eat.' He picked up the bucket and poured its contents into the trough. 'You'll have to clear up, Jo; I think you'll find that Isaac and Mr Hogan are going to be busy troubleshooting sick dragons for the next few days.'

Isaac, with Mr Hogan in tow, was whisked away later that morning in a WDRF van. Another two dragons had died that morning and four more were now seriously ill; including Emilia Chatfield's dragon, Tambourine Man.

As soon as they'd gone, everyone else met in the library to talk over events.

'Luckily only those dragons that came into direct contact with Nemesis have contracted the flu so far. Of course Aurora took the full brunt,' said Spiky Mike. 'I'll never forgive myself for putting her in harm's way like that.'

'Hey, man, you can't blame yourself,' said Hannibal generously. 'There's no way you could have known what would happen.'

'And you saved Dominic,' said Joanna. 'I think Aurora would have wanted that, don't you?'

'Talking of Dominic,' said Spiky Mike. 'DC Reese phoned to say he's all right, although he needed a few stitches in his head. His nan was badly shaken up from being imprisoned in a cave for so long, but otherwise she's fine. Why not give him a ring. I've got the number if you want it?'

'Thanks,' said Joanna turning away quickly because she could already feel herself starting to blush.

'He's a nice kid,' remarked Spiky Mike. 'Nice kid, but a terrible flyer! Don't you think?'

'Mike, leave her alone,' Afra nudged him.

'No, it's OK,' said Joanna. 'He is nice and he *is* a terrible flyer! I wonder what he'll do now.'

Spiky Mike suddenly looked thoughtful. 'What he needs is a good trainer – and a dragon that can fly in more than just a straight line.'

'And what you need, Mike,' insisted Afra, 'is to go home and get some sleep. You too, Joanna. You both look wrecked. Hannibal and I are quite capable of taking care of the caves for a couple of days.'

'But what about turning the egg?' protested Spiky Mike, as his girlfriend pushed him towards the door, 'Has it escaped your notice that we've lost our Egg Turner again and although I know the WDRF said they'd send a temporary Egg Turner, we really should be there to supervise them.'

'Just for once,' said Afra, 'let me worry about that.'

Spiky Mike admitted defeat and waved them goodbye with another huge yawn. As soon as he had gone Afra sighed.

'I hope you didn't mind my saying we'd look after the caves, Hannibal – it's obvious he's exhausted.'

Hannibal shrugged. 'It's good to be useful. What about you? Are you OK?'

Afra looked sadly at the flyer. 'It's just . . . I miss her so.'

Joanna stared at Afra in dismay. Of course – she'd

lost Aurora too. Marius King's revenge on his old dragon-racing team had been merciless. She tried hard not to think of him sitting there laughing at his success.

'At least Marius King hasn't won,' insisted Joanna.

'I'm sorry, Jo,' said Afra sadly. 'But I think you're wrong. His intention was to wreak havoc and he has! Of course it was a victory for us that Isaac managed to save Excelsior. But we mustn't forget that dragons have died. And what about their flyers and trainers? What are they going to do? What are *any* of us going to do?'

# 31
## RESOLVING
# THINGS

'There's a faulty valve on your firebox!' Mrs East, the WDRF replacement Egg Turner huffed her way into Afra's office. 'I would like it noted please in writing that any damage to the egg is not my responsibility.'

'A faulty valve?' said Afra rather taken aback, as she signed Mrs East's incident sheet. The woman had been a nightmare, always complaining about something!

'Yes!' replied Mrs East. 'Really, I think you should replace the whole firebox or it might go wrong again. For the moment I have put the egg in a temporary heated carrier.'

'And this faulty valve, it . . . ?' asked Afra, not knowing much about the technical details of fireboxes.

'Regulates the temperature of the egg of course.

And if it's not working, the temperature dial returns to its default setting,' replied Mrs East, as if Afra were some ignorant novice.

'Which is?' asked Afra, knowing she was exasperating Mrs East even more.

'The default setting is "Off", of course.'

The real meaning of her words suddenly dawned on Afra. 'Oh, Mrs East, but that's wonderful, *wonderful*!'

'What are you talking about?' Mrs East looked most put out by Afra's outburst.

Just then Hannibal came into the office.

'Hannibal, it's wonderful news!' Afra couldn't stop smiling. 'Mrs East had just told me that the valve that regulates the temperature on the firebox is faulty.'

It took Hannibal a couple of seconds to register what Afra had just told him, but then to Mrs East's amazement Hannibal suddenly whizzed her around. 'Mrs East, I could kiss you!'

She looked at him hopefully but when he didn't she said, with as much dignity as she could muster, 'I don't understand what's going on. So if you don't mind, I'll show you where I've put the egg and then I'll be off home.'

As soon as she had gone the pair of them both burst out laughing. 'Did you see her face? Goodness knows what she'll say to Sir John. Thank goodness Isaac will be back tomorrow.'

'I always knew Isaac didn't mess with that firebox,' sighed Hannibal with satisfaction. 'I just knew it!'

It was strange being back in the Brixton Caves, thought Isaac as he and Mr Hogan came down in the lift. They had only been away three days but already it felt like a lifetime. To his relief they hadn't lost any more dragons, although it had been touch and go with Tambourine Man at the Blackpool Caves. Thank goodness Mouse had phoned to let them know they had an emergency on their hands.

As they made their way to the offices, the caves seemed very quiet. Only Afra was around.

'You're back!' she beamed, seeing the pair of them. 'Goodbye and good riddance, Mrs East.'

'I don't think I've had the privilege of her acquaintance,' said Mr Hogan.

'Yeah, who is she?' asked Isaac.

'The WDRF replacement Egg Turner. A dreadful woman. However, Isaac, you will think her perfectly wonderful. Listen to this . . .'

Afra told him about the faulty valve and Isaac smiled in pure relief.

'I knew I hadn't done anything . . . although I'll have to apologise to Joanna.' Isaac looked rather embarrassed. 'Remember, I thought it was Dominic Pieterson all along!'

'Whoops!' said Afra. 'Well she's down with Excelsior if you want to get it over with.'

Isaac continued to look rather sheepish. 'Actually I think I'll phone Grandma instead.'

'Definitely an easier option,' said Afra handing him the phone. 'Give Agnes my love and tell her we're all looking forward to seeing her really soon.'

'Where is everyone else?' asked Mr Hogan. 'It's very quiet.'

'Mike and Hannibal are having a boys' day out,' said Afra. 'They were talking about going to the seaside!'

Joanna was genuinely pleased to see Mr Hogan when he arrived down in the cave to say hello.

'Mr Hogan, it's great to see you. Thank you so much for everything you've done. Look how well Excelsior is.'

'Me? I just followed a chemical formula. Isaac's the one who's saved the dragons,' said Mr Hogan, unwilling to accept the praise. 'And it's thanks to you that we had access to the manuscripts.'

'To think if I'd continued to be so pig-headed, Excelsior would have died.' Joanna gave a shudder at the thought. 'But what about you? Will Isaac be able to help you walk again?'

Mr Hogan looked sadly at Joanna. 'It doesn't

look likely. It seems the damage to the nerves in my spine is beyond repair.'

'I'm really sorry,' said Joanna, thinking Mr Hogan was being very brave about it.

'Don't be,' said Mr Hogan. 'I'm a lucky man. I have friends who care and a job I love – and I've just had the most extraordinary experience of helping an amazing young man save the lives of dying dragons. Have you seen Isaac yet? I know he wanted to visit Excelsior.'

'Not yet,' smiled Joanna.

'Well, I'm sure he'll be in soon,' said Mr Hogan, wheeling his chair back out of the cave.

Joanna knew why Isaac hadn't been to see Excelsior. He was avoiding her. As for herself, she wasn't at all sure what she would say to him when he did appear. He was the Alchemist – Vincent's heir. She was forever in his debt for saving her dragon.

'Just be yourself, JoJo,' Excelsior kept insisting.

'I'm afraid it's not that simple, XL,' said Joanna. 'I mean . . .'

'You were horrible to him before and now you feel guilty?' suggested Excelsior.

'All right, you don't need to rub it in. I know I need to apologise! Just give me time. At least until after tomorrow.' Joanna gave a shudder. 'Spiky Mike's called a big meeting for everyone. Even my mum and dad are coming, so it must be about something that affects me.'

'Ah,' said Excelsior. 'Do you think he's going to announce his future plans?'

'Yes,' moaned Joanna. 'But how can I work with any other trainer than him?'

# 32
## SPIKY MIKE'S
# NEWS

The town hall clock had just sounded nine as Joanna and her parents arrived at the caves. To Joanna, descending in the lift, they were nine heralds announcing her impending doom. She was feeling physically sick at the thought of the meeting.

As everyone gathered in the library, Joanna couldn't help but wonder if she was being paranoid or whether they all looked as if they knew something she didn't. Spiky Mike took his place at the head of the table. He was wearing a suit! And a tie! And he'd obviously had a shave.

*That's it then,* she thought, *he must be going to do some sort of little formal speech or something, saying what a wonderful time he's had blah, blah.* She slunk into a chair between Hannibal and Mr Hogan.

'Hi, everyone,' said Spiky Mike. 'First of all I'd like

to update you on the latest info as to the whereabouts of Marius King and Trix Dawson. It seems they're in South Africa. Apparently, Trix Dawson has *connexions* there. The police are now pursuing their enquires via Interpol and as soon as I hear anything else I'll let you know. In the meantime I've got a very important announcement to make.' Spiky Mike hesitated and gave a nervous cough.

*Here it comes*, thought Joanna. She could feel her legs shaking under the table. She didn't want to look at him when he broke the news, so she sat there staring at her hands in her lap.

'Actually – Afra, do you want to tell everyone?' said Spiky Mike suddenly.

'No!' Afra seemed horrified. 'I want to hear you say it – you can't go back on your word now, you know.'

If she'd been looking, Joanna would have seen Spiky Mike take Afra's hand.

'Hmm,' he coughed again.

'Come on, man,' groaned Hannibal. 'We all know what you're going to say.'

Joanna looked up. Why was everybody smiling?

'Afra and I would like to announce our engagement!' said Spiky Mike proudly.

'WHOO-HOO! About time too,' said Hannibal. He nudged Joanna. 'He asked her at the Valentine Chase.'

Joanna didn't know what to say, she had been expecting such a different kind of announcement – concerning herself – that she felt a little bewildered by it all. Of course it was great news, but then everyone had always known they would get engaged sooner or later, hadn't they? Perhaps it was going to be a case of good news first, like some sort of sweetener to get everyone on his side. Oh if only he'd get round to telling her her fate.

'Thank you,' smiled Spiky Mike. 'Well that was my first announcement. Next . . .'

Joanna held her breath.

'Yesterday Hannibal and I went down to visit the Brighton Caves. As you know, the lease is up for sale, so Hannibal, Afra and I have decided to buy it between us. Our plan is to set up a dragon flying school. We're inundated by requests from young flyers desperate to get a good training – look at Dominic Pieterson. Of course it will take time. The caves would have to be adapted and modernised, and we'd have to provide proper educational facilities. Ambrose, we would be especially grateful for your input there.'

Mr Hogan looked overwhelmed.

'Thank you, I'd be delighted. Goodness a whole school curriculum to organise. I'd better get planning.'

'What about dragons?' said Isaac excitedly. 'We'll need to start turning some more eggs. I was talking to

Mr Chatfield when I was up in Blackpool and he has a couple of female dragons getting ready to lay.'

'Fantastic,' said Spiky Mike. 'We need as many people to come on board to help us as possible.'

Joanna couldn't believe her ears. He was going to train other young flyers! In Brighton! She sat there stunned, unable to speak. This was far worse than she'd imagined.

'That's all really,' said Spiky Mike. 'Except to say I have an appointment this afternoon with Sir John and our solicitor to finalise the conditions of the lease.'

*That's explains the suit*, thought Joanna.

Everybody got up and went out busily discussing all the news. Anthony and Hilary Morris seemed just as excited about the school as everyone else. They kissed their daughter goodbye and hurried off to work. Joanna found herself alone in the library.

*That's that then. Spiky Mike, Afra and Hannibal are setting up a school and everyone else is going to help them.* But what about the Brixton Caves? *Her* caves! What on earth was *she* going to do? Perhaps her dad would drive her to the races and her mum could do the paperwork. XL didn't seem to think they needed a trainer, but if necessary she was sure Giovanni would help her find someone.

Joanna looked around the library. She remembered Spiky Mike on that first visit she'd ever made to the caves, sitting there looking so out of place in his jeans and T-shirt. Just the memory of it made her cry. She couldn't help it. Suddenly the door opened and in came . . . Spiky Mike! Joanna quickly wiped her face so he couldn't see her tears.

'Forgot my briefcase,' he said, and then stopped. 'Joanna, what's the matter? Why are you crying?'

She looked up at him and the inevitable flare of anger that he always seemed to provoke in her made her snap.

'Why couldn't you just say you aren't going to be my trainer any more, instead of wrapping it up in all your plans about a new school?'

'What are you talking about?' asked Spiky Mike, looking in bewilderment at his young flyer. 'Who said I wasn't going to train you any more?'

'You walked out!' Joanna accused him.

'You said you wanted Afra to be your trainer,' replied Spiky Mike rather justifiably.

'Well I've changed my mind. I don't know what I'd have done if you hadn't disobeyed the WDRF and brought Excelsior back to Brixton . . .'

'Yeah, that may be, but I still haven't got over the fact that I led you straight to Marius King. That wasn't my cleverest decision.'

'You didn't know he'd be there,' said Joanna.

Spike Mike nodded. 'I guess not. But it certainly

wasn't the only mistake I made. I should have believed you about losing the race.'

Joanna could hardly believe her ears. Spiky Mike was apologising! But all she said was, 'I think I understand why you were so upset about me and Dominic.'

Spiky Mike gave her a surprised look.

'Mr Hogan said you acted like that because it had reminded you of when your sister died.'

'Perhaps it did,' said Spiky Mike wistfully. 'You remind me of her . . . a lot. So that's all the more reason for me to be your trainer.'

'But Giovanni said . . .'

'Sounds like a lot of people have been talking,' interrupted Spiky Mike. 'Look, Jo, after all we've been through did you seriously think I would let anyone else train you? I wouldn't want them to take the glory,' he added mischievously.

Joanna felt light and giddy with relief. 'Excelsior said that we – I mean *he* – didn't really need a trainer. That you'd taught us too well.'

'Did he now?' laughed Spiky Mike. 'Well you can tell him from me that he's starting to overarch his neck in his takeoff and I'm devising a particularly long and onerous exercise to put it right.'

'But how will you train me and run a school?' asked Joanna, still not sure whether to laugh or cry with relief. 'Even you can't be in two places at once.'

'The school won't open for quite some time yet – at least for another eighteen months! But we need to secure the lease now, before someone else snaps it up – dragon caves don't come up for sale every day! When the school starts, Afra will do the day-to-day training. I'll just run master classes, using you to show our new flyers how it's done.

'*Really?*' said Joanna.

'Really!' said Spiky Mike. 'Why do I always have to remind you that you're World Champion?' He picked up the briefcase from next to his chair. 'Oh, there was one thing I didn't say in the meeting. I didn't want to embarrass you in front of everyone. How would you feel if Dominic had a few lessons with us in the holidays? Of course he'll need to get a dragon to fly first. I really need to teach him how to take off properly – it's been driving me crazy every time I've had to watch it.'

'Me too,' said Joanna, wiping her nose for the hundredth time on her now very soggy tissue.

'Look, I really must go. I don't want to be late and get in Sir John's bad books – I'm still waiting for him to sanction fireballing. And after that I'm taking Afra shopping for a ring.'

'No wonder you're wearing a suit,' laughed Joanna.

The Trustees of the Brixton Dragon Caves
are delighted to request the presence of

Joanna Morris

on 25$^{th}$ February
at the Royal Pavilion, Brighton

to celebrate
the engagement of Afra Power and Michael Hill,
the memorial of the first anniversary
of Vincent Marlowe
and the second birthday of Excelsior

7 pm Unveiling of memorial plaque
followed by
Excelsior's Birthday Cake
7.30 pm Drinks
8 pm Dinner
Dancing till late

RSVP

261

# 33
## THE ROYAL
# PAVILION

'Come on, Mouse, the taxi's going to be here soon,' shouted Joanna. 'Are you nearly ready?'

'Coming,' shouted Mouse, throwing open the bathroom door. 'I'm just making the most of not having to share a bathroom with all my sisters. And don't you just love Brighton?'

'Isn't it the same as Blackpool?' asked Joanna.

'A bit, but I don't get to stay in a hotel with my best friend in Blackpool,' laughed Mouse. 'Or get to dress up for swanky parties in a Royal Pavilion! Now tell me the truth – do I look OK?'

Joanna had to admit Mouse looked terrific.

'I *love* your silver leggings; they're just like the ones we wore for the fashion shoot at Ms Lupin's.'

'That's because they *are* the leggings. I phoned her and asked if I could borrow them. Ooh and that reminds me, Ms Lupin said the fashion shoot will be in next month's edition of *Dragon Fire*. I can't wait. I wonder if we'll be pin-ups on anyone's wall?'

Joanna went and stood in front of the mirror. 'You don't think I look a bit frumpy in this dress? My mum insisted I wore it.'

'No, it's really pretty,' said Mouse. 'Just a bit long, hitch it up a bit over that belt thing . . . that's much better. Anyway, at least you know Dominic will ask you to dance.'

'Do you think so?' asked Joanna nervously. 'I mean I don't want to have to rely on my mum telling my brother he's got to dance with me. It would be so embarrassing.'

'Of course he will. Come on, Jo, he really likes you! Anyway I'm not going to wait to be asked. If they don't ask me, I'm going to ask them.'

'Them?' said Joanna, shocked. 'There's more than one!'

'Well, of course I want to dance with Hannibal, but then I do know he's invited Niamh . . .'

'Who told you that?' asked Joanna, always intrigued by how Mouse knew all the gossip.

'She rang Emilia to ask what she was wearing and I overheard their conversation – Emilia always talks so loud, I couldn't help it!'

'Who else do you want to dance with then?'

'Isaac! He's the hero of the hour. I really liked him when he came up to save Tambourine Man. Afterwards we went and had fish and chips together on the beach and he's brilliant at football.'

'He used to be in the team with my brother,' said Joanna. 'He gave it up when he became Egg Turner.' *And an alchemist who saved Excelsior,* she added silently.

Isaac was still proving to be a problem for Joanna. He avoided her and she avoided him. Joanna was relieved that for tonight, at least, Mouse would take care of him.

By the time they arrived, the Pavilion Music Room, where the party was to be held, was already filling up with guests. It was very strange seeing everyone dressed up in their finery. Most strange of all was seeing Spiky Mike and Giovanni in dinner jackets and bow ties. They didn't seem quite real! But then Joanna saw someone who really was real – someone she'd wanted to see for ages. She seemed much smaller than Joanna remembered and so much older.

'Agnes!' cried Joanna and ran over and threw her arms around her. 'I'm so glad you're here.'

'I wouldn't have missed it for the world,' smiled the old Egg Turner. 'Tonight, I remember my old friend the Alchemist and I welcome the new.'

Joanna followed her gaze across the room. Isaac

was standing surrounded by official dignitaries from the WDRF, who were all shaking his hand. Suddenly she caught his eye. Immediately he turned away.

Joanna looked back at Agnes, hoping she hadn't noticed and said quickly, 'The Pavilion is amazing. I can't believe I've never been here before.'

But Agnes, despite her failing health had not missed anything. 'I'm sorry you and Isaac aren't good friends. I can't help but think you're supposed to be.'

Before Joanna could reply, Spiky Mike started loudly inviting everyone to the Brighton Caves so that the memorial to Vincent could take place. 'And after that we'll all wish Excelsior a happy birthday.'

It was a silent solemn gathering that remembered how exactly one year ago to that very day Vincent Marlowe had sacrificed himself to save his young dragon flyer. *From Marius King!* thought Joanna shuddering.

She tried to push him out of her thoughts but he would not go. They'd outwitted him this time, but she knew he was still out there, plotting, biding his time, waiting for an opportunity to get her . . . and Excelsior.

Excelsior was completely well again. There wasn't a trace of the illness; in fact, he was stronger than ever; a sleek and shining silver racing dragon. Standing so close to him, Joanna could feel the fire in his belly twisting and curling. He seemed strangely content to be back in the caves where such dreadful events had happened.

'But it's not the caves that matter,' said Excelsior, interrupting her thoughts. 'It's the people and dragons who live here. And this is it, a new beginning. Look, a cave full of our friends!'

Joanna looked at the faces watching Agnes as she unveiled the small plaque in memory of Vincent. XL was right. They had so many friends – Spiky Mike, Afra, Hannibal, Mouse, Giovanni, Lucia, Ms Lupin, Agnes, Dominic – why even Mr Hogan!

'What about Isaac?' she heard Excelsior mutter. 'I mean he saved me *and* he's the Alchemist . . .'

'OK! OK!' frowned Joanna. 'I do know.'

'So apologise,' insisted Excelsior. 'Make it my birthday present!'

Ironically it was Isaac who brought the birthday cake over to the presentation table for Joanna to give to Excelsior in front of all the guests. Neither of them looked at each other. Instead they made a huge fuss of Excelsior, who promptly ignored them both.

Soon after Excelsior's cake all the guests started to make their way back to the Pavilion Music Room, until there was only Isaac and Joanna left.

'I don't mind settling Excelsior in his cave,' said Isaac brusquely. 'I'm sure your friends are waiting for you.'

Before Joanna could reply, Excelsior give her a quick look that meant only one thing.

She stood there for a moment remembering Isaac as she had seen him in the silver light of the fire.

'Actually, Isaac . . .' she started to say.

'What, what is it, Joanna?'

'I just wanted . . .'

'Look, if you want to settle Excelsior yourself, just say so. I know it's his birthday . . .'

'ISAAC, I'M TRYING TO SAY SORRY,' Joanna shouted in exasperation. 'Don't make it any harder . . . No! That's not how I wanted to say it.'

Joanna came and stood close to Excelsior, resting her hand on his neck. 'What I really wanted to say was that I'm sorry. Sorry that I've been so horrid to you – and after you saved Excelsior – but that's not why I'm sorry. I'm sorry because I was jealous . . . I mean,' continued Joanna. 'Agnes is *your* grandma, and you're really good at Latin and . . . I know XL really likes you.'

Isaac nodded. 'Yeah well, perhaps I was jealous too. I mean you're World Champion and you fly Excelsior and have friends who understand about dragons.'

They both stood there for a moment not sure what else to say.

It was Isaac who continued. 'Actually, I should

really apologise to Dominic. He didn't sabotage the egg.'

'He didn't?' said Joanna in surprise.

'Apparently it was a faulty valve on the firebox. I should have told you sooner.'

'OK!' snorted Excelsior. 'Apologies made and accepted, although it took you both long enough. So now – about *me!* I would quite like a little sleep after all that cake. I mean I'm a whole year older than yesterday and I need to rest more.'

Joanna and Isaac both laughed.

'You go on up, Joanna,' said Isaac. 'I really don't mind settling Excelsior tonight. You don't want to get your dress dirty and everyone's waiting for you.'

'You *are* coming up though?' asked Joanna.

'Of course,' said Isaac. 'As long as I don't have to talk to that dreadful Sir John. He keeps calling me over to congratulate me on saving the dragon-racing world, when what he really means is I got him off the hook.'

'Come and sit with us, we have a secret weapon to set on him if he gets too troublesome.'

Isaac looked at her blankly. 'A secret weapon?'

'She's called Mouse,' laughed Joanna as she started to climb the stairs. 'Although I think she'd rather talk to you.'

'Thanks, Joanna,' smiled Isaac. 'I'll see you later.'

Joanna looked back to watch Isaac lead her dragon

down the passageway. She could see the silver fire glowing around them both in the darkness; the Alchemist and the dragon.

*Actually*, thought Joanna, *I think I'd like to talk to you too*. She gave a little smile and called out, 'Hey, Isaac, it's Jo . . . my friends call me Jo!'

For more information about the
*Dragon Racer* series or to find out about
other great Catnip titles go to:

**www.catnippublishing.co.uk**